A FIX LIKE THIS

A FIX LIKE THIS

A Mario Balzic Mystery

K.C. Constantine

MYSTERIOUSPRESS.COM

All rights reserved, including without limitation the right to reproduce this book or any portion thereof in any form or by any means, whether electronic or mechanical, now known or hereinafter invented, without the express written permission of the publisher.

This is a work of fiction. Names, characters, places, events, and incidents either are the product of the author's imagination or are used fictitiously. Any resemblance to actual persons, living or dead, businesses, companies, events, or locales is entirely coincidental.

Copyright © 1975 by K.C. Constantine

ISBN: 978-1-5040-9156-5

This edition published in 2024 by MysteriousPress.com/Open Road Integrated Media, Inc.
180 Maiden Lane
New York, NY 10038
www.openroadmedia.com

A FIX LIKE THIS

Balzic waited for the woman to be done. She was in her sixties, her white hair grew in tight curls, and she smelled of garlic. Her floral print housedress was ripped under both arms. Though she'd been talking to the admissions clerk for nearly five minutes, she was still shivering from the cold. She'd obviously left her home too quickly to think of wearing a coat or sweater.

The admissions clerk explained twice to the woman how to file for government health insurance for her husband, who had been conscious but torpid when he was wheeled into the Emergency Unit of Conemaugh General Hospital. Except for her shivering now, the woman seemed calm enough, though every time she asked a question, she put her hand to her mouth and her fingers trembled.

When she'd asked every question she could think of, she turned away from the counter and said aloud to herself, "My God, what am I going to do now?" Then she turned back abruptly to the counter, bumping Balzic with her hip. "Can I go be with him? I'm allowed ain't I? My mister, he's all I got."

"Certainly," the clerk said. "Through those doors on your right. Mrs. Havrilak will show you where he is."

The woman bumped Balzic again as she turned away from

the counter and hurried, her bosom heaving, through the fire doors leading to the treatment rooms.

"May I help you?" the clerk said.

Balzic held out his ID case because the clerk was new to him. "I got a call about a stabbing a while ago, and I got tied up in something or I would've been here sooner. Who do I talk to about it?"

"Dr. Kamil, I think. He's the very dark-complected one. Just go through those doors—"

"I know where to go," Balzic said. "I just wanted a name."

He pushed through the fire doors and walked past treatment rooms on both sides until he came to the office. Off to his right he could hear a youngster bawling and a woman cooing reassurances. In another of the rooms a man was swearing quietly about a foot, probably his, though he was cursing about it as though it belonged to somebody else, somebody not very smart.

The office was empty. Balzic took a seat at one of the desks and waited. Shortly, a tall, freckle-faced nurse appeared in the doorway. She fumbled through her pockets while staring at the floor, then stepped quickly to one of the other desks and began to pat with both hands on papers jumbled on it. Only then did she notice Balzic, and she smiled brightly.

"Mario! How are you? I haven't seen you in a month of bad Saturday nights."

"Hello, Louise. How's business?"

"Listen, go get a lab coat. Some of these people you could take care of. I don't know where they came from today. God." She found what she'd been looking for and held it up for Balzic to see. "Around here, pens are more precious than blood." She started out the door but stopped short. "You waiting to see Kamil about the guy who was stabbed?"

Balzic nodded.

"I'll tell him you're here. He's just finishing up with some sutures. At least I hope he is. God, is he slow. I could put a zipper in a dress in the time it takes him to do ten stitches."

"He the only one on duty?"

"No, but the other one's right out of school. Last week, I think. I gotta go," she said, her crepe soles squishing as she broke into a trot.

Balzic took out his keychain and opened the nail clipper and began to clean his fingernails. He pared them over an ashtray, looking up every time he heard footsteps, but none turned into the office.

He closed the clipper and put his keys away and waited some more, looking around the office, mildly curious for a time about a poison chart under glass on the desk where he was sitting. He had just started to read the antidote for copperhead venom when a slight, short man in a lab coat came in. His brilliantly black hair grew in swirls and came very near to his eyebrows.

"I'm Dr. Kamil," he said. His accent was Middle Eastern, Syrian perhaps or Lebanese. "You are the chief of police?"

Balzic introduced himself and shook hands with the doctor. He could not remember shaking a man's hand so delicate.

"Ah, yes. So. What do you want to know?" The doctor clipped his words and spoke rapidly in a thin, tenor voice.

"Whatever you can tell me."

"I have the record here. Yes. So. Here it is. The patient is male, Caucasian, forty years of age, and very, very obese. If his brother had not been here to assist us, I do not think we are able to place him on the cart. His brother is also very obese. I have never seen such obesity as you have here in America. But these two brothers are beyond even my belief. Still in all—is that how you say that? Still in all? You have so many idioms here too—"

"Was the guy's name Manditti?" Balzic interrupted.

"Say again please?"

"Manditti. His name."

Dr. Kamil peered at his report. "Yes. Armand. Italian no doubt."

"And his brother brought him in?"

"I suppose yes. I do not know."

"No police officers came with them?"

"I did not see any."

"Where is he now?"

"In surgery most certainly."

"How long ago did he go up?"

"Thirty minutes, more or less."

"Was he conscious? Did he say anything?"

"Oh yes, he was conscious. But he was cursing and crying. If not for his brother to assist us, we would have no information at all."

"Did his brother go upstairs with him?"

"I suppose yes. I do not know."

"All right, Doctor," Balzic said. "Thank you. I'd appreciate it if you'd have somebody type up a report as soon as possible. Mrs. Havrilak knows about the forms and what to put on them. Thanks again."

"There is no need to thank me. It is my duty, is it not?"

"Yeah, but thanks anyway," Balzic said. He shook the doctor's hand, reminding himself not to squeeze.

As soon as the doctor left the office, Balzic picked up a phone on one of the desks and dialed Troop A Barracks of the Pennsylvania State Police.

"State police, Sergeant Rudawski."

"Rudi, this is Balzic. Who's in charge of CID now?"

"Johnson."

"He is? I thought he was going to be transferred out as soon as Minyon passed his physical."

"Well, put an extra quarter in the collection this Sunday, 'cause Minyon flunked his physical, and he is, as they say, being retired with honor." The ironic pleasure in Rudawski's voice was unmistakable.

"Oh beautiful," Balzic said, laughing. "Just beautiful. Well, let me talk to Johnson."

"Hold on." There was a click, then a dead sound, then another click.

"Criminal Investigation Division, Lieutenant Johnson."

"Hey, Walker, old buddy, congratulations. Rudi just told me Shitface flunked his physical and you're going to be with us for a while longer. That's the best news I heard today."

"Mario? Yeah. It looks that way. I almost feel bad for him though. That's a hell of a slice off his pension."

"Don't waste your sympathy. Even his mother had to know he was hopeless," Balzic said. "Listen, Walk, I got a problem. A guy was stabbed. His brother brought him to the hospital, and nobody reported it. I mean, the hospital people called me. And I know them, so it figures they wouldn't report it themselves. But I'm also taking a pretty good guess that it happened pretty close to home. What I'd like is for you to take your people over there and see if I'm right and see what you can come up with, okay?"

"No problem," Johnson said. "From the way you said it I take it he's not dead."

"Yeah, but he's still in surgery so I don't really know what kind of shape he's in. I'm on my way up there now. But listen, don't bother trying to ask any of the neighbors up there anything. They still haven't figured out this isn't Sicily. They see those uniforms, they'll forget how to speak English. Just do a job on the house, okay?"

"Okay, what's the address?"

"You remember where Norwood Hill is?"

"Yeah."

"Well, it's the last house on the right on Norwood Hill Road. Never mind about a number. It sort of sits off by itself. It used to be a half-decent house when their old man was alive, but there's just the two brothers living there now and they're both slobs."

"What's the name?"

"Manditti. Armand is the victim. He's a runner and gofer for Muscotti. His brother's name is Tullio. He runs Muscotti's dump. Couple of real beauties. They call the one Fat Manny and the other one Tullio the Tub. You'd need a truck scale to weigh them."

"Okay, Mario. I'll see what we can do, and I'll let you know."

"Really appreciate it, Walk. Just remember that I'm guessing. It could've happened anywhere. Thanks, buddy."

Balzic hung up and then made his way to the main elevators and up to the seventh floor, where the operating and recovery rooms were, waiting in the corridor by the nurses' station. He looked around for Tullio Manditti but did not see him. Off to his left in an adjoining corridor he could hear a woman mumbling and giggling in that euphoria brought on by preoperative chemicals. Nurses in green surgical caps and gowns bustled about. A doctor in street clothes got off one of the elevators and hurried past Balzic, stripping off his tie as he disappeared through fire doors on the right.

Presently, a plump, middle-aged nurse in white appeared from yet a third corridor. She carried a cup of tea and smiled at Balzic. He held up his ID case, but she waved it away.

"I know who you are," she said. "And you want to know about Mr. Manditti, right?"

"You're a good thing," Balzic said. "What else you going to tell me so I don't have to ask?"

"Well, Dr. Ayoub did the work and he was assisted by Dr.

Mitchell. They finished about five minutes ago. I'll go get Ayoub for you."

"Wait a second. Where's Manditti's brother?"

"Oh, God, he smelled up the place so bad I told him to leave. He wasn't supposed to be up here anyway. I told him to go home and change clothes. But the way he was carrying on, he probably didn't. He's probably downstairs in the lobby driving everybody crazy."

"He was still in his work clothes?"

"Well, I hope he doesn't sit around the house like that. Where's he work anyway?"

"Where could you work and smell like that? A dump. Excuse me. Sanitary landfills they call them now."

A doctor in surgical clothes appeared then, thin, short, very dark, his black hair glistening from perspiration. "You are from the police?"

Balzic nodded.

"I'm Dr. Ayoub."

"Where they getting all you Syrians and Lebanese?" Balzic said, laughing.

"From Syria and Lebanon, I suppose," the doctor said. His smile was forced.

"Well, uh, yeah. I guess they would," Balzic said and coughed. The nurse busied herself with some charts.

"So what can you tell me, Doc?"

"He had nine wounds, all of them simple puncture wounds except for two. Those were made presumably by the blade being thrust in and then pulled down. Like so." The doctor demonstrated on Balzic's chest. "The instrument was not very large. None of the wounds was deeper than six inches. The procedure was simple."

"He's going to live?"

"Oh yes. Barring infection, which is unlikely, he will die of heart disease. But for the time being his obesity saved him. It required every nurse in all three rooms to lift him onto the table. And off again."

"How long will he be in the recovery room?"

"How long before you will be able to talk with him sensibly?"

"Yeah, I guess that's what I mean."

"The anesthesia was very mild. We were concerned about his blood pressure. Forty-five minutes. Perhaps not even that long."

"Uh, Doc, would any of those wounds have been fatal to somebody built like me or you?"

"It's difficult to say. Most were in the area of the heart. Two were lower, near the stomach. To someone built like me, surely four or five would have been lethal, that is to say, each of four or five."

"So somebody wasn't just trying to cut him up. Somebody was trying to kill him."

"As I said, if the wounds had been inflicted on me I would be dead. Whether someone was trying to kill him is, I think, your department."

"Can you tell me anything about the kind of weapon?"

"Some kind of simple knife blade. No more than six inches. But I can say nothing more specific than that. I am a resident in general surgery, not in forensic pathology."

"Sure, I understand. Well, thank you very much."

"You're welcome. Good day," Dr. Ayoub said, turning at once and walking briskly away.

Balzic looked at the nurse, who was trying not to smile. "I guess I didn't score too many points with him."

"Oh, he's all right," the nurse said. "He's just all business."

Balzic thanked her and went with a wave over his shoulder to the elevators. In the lobby he looked around, trying to locate

Tullio Manditti, but he didn't see him. Balzic approached one of the hospital security guards and held out his ID case. The guard nodded.

"You seen a short, fat guy, really fat, in dirty clothes?"

"In the coffee shop, feeding his face—as if he needs it. He chased everybody out."

"Coffee shop still in the same place? Every time I come up here they're moving things around, putting on all these additions and wings."

"Well, they haven't moved that yet. But give them time. They will."

"Yeah. So how's it going? They treating you all right?"

"No use complaining."

"Okay, pal, take it easy." Balzic oriented himself and then set off for the coffee shop. He found Tullio Manditti more than occupying a stool at the counter. Both waitresses were smoking in the farthest corner away from Tullio and whispering to each other, their eyes darting toward Tullio as he took a third of a glazed doughnut in one bite. One of the waitresses asked Balzic if she could help him.

"Just coffee. Black." He took a stool two away from Tullio. He wouldn't have sat closer to Tullio if he'd been able to.

"Tullio, why didn't you go home and take a bath and get cleaned up like the people asked you?"

Tullio stuffed the rest of the doughnut in his mouth in two bites and chewed rapidly. He turned to look at Balzic but spoke to the waitresses. "Give me two more. And another milk shake."

"We don't have any more doughnuts."

"You got any pie?"

"Just apple and cherry."

"I hate apple and cherry. Ain't you got no banana cream?"

"No."

"Then forget the pie. Give me a couple cheeseburgers with everything. Extra onions. And grill the onions." Tullio had been looking at Balzic while he spoke to the waitress. Now he turned back to the milk shake container in front of him. He looked inside, sloshed the last of the liquid around, and drank directly from it, letting out a thunderous belch when he finished.

"What did you say, Balzic?"

"You heard me."

"Why don't I go home and take a bath, huh? Is that what you said?"

"That's what I said."

"So tell the people to give their garbage a bath, don't tell me. Tell them to put deodorant on their garbage, then maybe I don't smell, how's that? Huh? What's the matter with you, Balzic? You stupid or something? My brother's up there dying and you want me to leave here and go home and get a bath, Cheesus."

"Well, I see it didn't interfere with your appetite."

"Eating, my brother understands. But going home and taking a bath, he wouldn't understand. He'd never forgive me."

"Come off it, Tullio. Your brother's not dying. Not yet anyway. He'll croak from a heart attack pretty soon, just like you. But he's not dying from those holes he got in him."

"That's what you say. Huh! What do you know? You some kind of doctor?"

"I just talked to the doctor. He'll live."

"When the doc tells me I'll believe it. What you tell me I stick up my gazoomey."

"Have it your way," Balzic said, shrugging. "So what happened?"

"What do I know what happened? I come home from work and there he was, bleeding all over the porch. Blood all over the living room, Cheesus."

"And you didn't talk to him about it?"

"What talk, you kiddin'? I'm trying to save him, I ain't worrying about no conversation."

"So how'd you get him here? He had to be conscious. You couldn't have brought him here if he's unconscious."

"So he was conscious a little bit."

"Conscious enough to walk, right?"

"Look, Balzic, I can see where you're going. If he's conscious enough to walk, he got to be conscious enough to talk. But I ain't asking him nothing. I'm just telling him to be cool, don't exert himself, we'll be there in a couple minutes."

"And naturally, that's what he did."

"That's exactly what he did."

"He didn't say one word about what happened or who or how or why?"

"He didn't say nothing."

"Okay. So he didn't say anything. So tell me what he's been doing lately."

"He ain't doing nothing. He's unemployed."

"What? He don't carry bags around for Dom Muscotti anymore?"

"What bags? Dom who?"

"Will you stop it. Who're you talking to? This is me, Tullio. And I know you and your brother since you were in Mother of Sorrows Elementary. You're not talking to some state horse or the FBI. I know how long you and your brother been working for Dom and I know what you do, so don't give my head a pain, all right?"

"I'm telling you my brother is unemployed."

"Wait a minute, what is this? You trying to tell me your brother doesn't pick up and deliver for Dom Muscotti anymore?"

"How many ways I got to say it? Cheesus."

"Tullio, you know just as soon as I leave here I'll go straight to Dom and ask him."

"I can't stop you from going nowhere."

"What happened with Dom and your brother?"

"What're you asking me for? What do I look like—the labor relations board? I don't know nothing about it."

"Tullio, that's two lies. You tell me one more I'm going to bust you as a material witness, and then I'll go to the DA and tell him you need to be locked up for your own safety. I can fix it so you stay in the slam for six months."

"You got to have a hearing before that, Balzic. Don't shit me."

"Hey, Tullio, you think I don't know the magistrates in this town? You think I can't have a hearing postponed as long as I want? You think about it, Tullio. And while you're at it, think about something else. Think about those twenty-two hundred calories you'll get every day down at the hotel . . . and lookee here. Here comes your milk shake."

Tullio sneered and swiveled around slightly on his stool, the plastic and metal creaking. He started to say something in Italian.

Balzic waved his index finger from side to side. "Easy, Tullio, easy. You don't want to say anything you're going to have to apologize for."

"What was I going to say? Was I going to say something, huh? Me? Nah. I was going to ask you to loan me a deuce, that's all. I'm a little short, and I didn't want to make no speech for the United Nations. So now you made me make one anyhow."

Balzic snorted and shook his head. He brought his money out, stripped off two bills, and pushed them toward Tullio. He stood and said, "Don't even thank me. Just go home and get cleaned up. Your brother'll understand. And everybody here'll love you."

Tullio drank his milk shake and seemed to be thinking, but he said nothing and did not look up as Balzic walked out.

Balzic debated with himself in the lobby whether to try to talk to Armand Manditti or to go straight to Dom Muscotti. An elevator opening in front of him made up his mind as much as anything else did. He rode up to the seventh floor, there holding the door open with one hand and calling out to the nurse he'd talked to earlier. "Is Manditti out of recovery yet?"

"He's on the third floor."

Balzic waved, stepped back inside the elevator, and pushed the button for three. Once there, he asked at the nurses' station for the room number. On his way, he chatted briefly with one of the charwomen, a friend of his mother's.

He found Armand Manditti in the first bed inside the door of a ward with four other beds, all empty. Balzic stopped in the doorway and laughed. The mound of white on the bed gave him the feeling that he was going to try to talk to a snow drift.

He stepped inside and saw Manny staring sleepily at the tube taped to the back of his hand. Manny blinked incredulously, the blinks coming very slowly. Every time his eyes opened, they would roll, and then Manny would shake his enormous head slowly from side to side, once each way.

"Manny? You hear me?"

"Huh? Am I dead?" The words came as ponderously as his blinks.

"You're not dead, Manny. At least you don't look it."

"Huh? Good . . . I'm glad . . . I thought I'm dead. . . ."

"Who stabbed you, Manny?"

Manny muttered something and closed his eyes and let out a long sigh. Balzic started to ask again, but Manny's sigh had turned into a snore and then another. Balzic took off his raincoat and threw it across the foot of the opposite bed. He looked around for an ashtray, found one, and then settled onto a straight-backed chair just inside the door. He smoked and hoped Manny wouldn't stay under the effect of the anesthetic too much longer.

He should have known better. An hour later, he was still waiting. He had talked to some nurses, then briefly to Dr. Ayoub, who had stopped on his way home. Manny continued to snore, the mattress, springs, and sheets groaning and rustling with each breath. Balzic inspected the bed and then the others in the room. Manny's bed was the same as the rest, and Balzic wondered how long it could take the strain.

Balzic could hear Tullio coming as soon as the elevator doors closed. With each heavy step came a breath as heavy. Tullio, freshly shaved and wearing clean coveralls, huffed into the room carrying a paper shopping bag. He stopped upon seeing Balzic and rolled his eyes toward the ceiling.

"Cheesus Christ, Balzic, state cops all over the house and you here. Whose idea was that—them state cops, huh? Yours? What's the big fuckin' idea? They come in there, they didn't have no search warrant or nothing."

"They don't need one."

"What do you mean, they don't need one? You cops can't just go busting into people's houses. Us people got some rights."

"Tullio, don't make my ass tired, okay? Don't say stupid things."

"Don't make my ass tired. Don't say stupid things." Tullio mimicked him, looking around for a place to put the shopping bag, deciding finally on the dining table at the foot of his brother's bed.

Out of it he took a loaf of Italian bread, two long pieces of pepperoni, a thick slab of provolone cheese, a jar of green olives stuffed with pearl onions, a can of black olives, a jar of banana peppers, and a transparent half-gallon bottle with no labels on it that obviously contained wine. Then he brought out a folded dish towel and opened it up. A small paring knife, a can opener, and a fork rolled out. Tullio took those and the towel and put them in the drawer in the stand beside his brother's bed. He looked around, as though thinking where to put the food.

"Tullio, why don't you just eat it yourself? Your brother's not going to be allowed to eat anything like that for a couple days."

"That's how much you know, Balzic. I know what you get in this place. I been here. You can die in here from the food. Half the cooks are niggers. When they find out the food's for a white person, they spit in it. You think I don't know that? They bring up a lunger, a real oyster, and they let you have it. My brother ain't eating in here, period."

"I don't know, Tullio," Balzic said, smiling. "I can remember the time Manny scarfed up seven barbecued chickens in about an hour. That was at the Sons of Italy picnic a couple years ago. Looks like all you brought him was a snack."

"Don't sweat your head, Balzic. My brother'll do okay in here, I'll take care of that."

"Tullio, Tullio. . . ." Manny's eyes opened wide.

"I'm here, Manny. Right here. What do you need?"

"Oh, Tullio, I ain't dead . . . that prick . . . I thought I'm dead."

"What prick, Manny?" Balzic said, going immediately to Manny's side.

"Aw take a hike, Balzic, willya!" Tullio said. "Can't you see he don't know what he's saying? Everybody's delirious when they wake up for crissake, everybody knows that . . . listen, Manny, don't try to talk. You just get some rest, okay? I'm here now. I brought you something to eat when you wake up. But keep sleeping now. You need it. You look bad, Manny. You look all green and yellow. You got to sleep that crap out of your system— that crap they put you out with. Just keep sleeping."

"Okay, okay. Just give me some water, okay? My throat's dry."

"Sure. How 'bout some wine in it? It'll make you sleep better."

"Yeah, sure . . . wine too. . . ."

"You better ask a nurse before you give him any wine, Tullio. It might make him really sick if it doesn't mix right with the anesthetic."

"What do you know? Go on, Balzic, take a walk. You don't think I know my brother's system better than any nurse? Go on, hit the bricks. You're making him nervous. Me too." Tullio peeled the wrapper off a glass, filled it half with wine, and added a little water. He rooted through the drawer of the bedstand behind him until he found a flexible straw. "Here, Manny, here you go. Take a couple big sips. It'll do you good. Really make you sleep good."

Manny raised his head and grimaced. "Holy shit, it hurts. . . ."

"Don't raise up. This straw bends. You don't have to raise up. Just lay there. I'll put the straw in your mouth . . . there, like that. See? Listen to Tullio. He'll take care of it."

"You going to take care of who did it too?" Balzic said.

"Listen, Balzic, I told you to take a hike. He don't have to say nothing and neither do I."

Balzic laughed. "Tullio, you been in trouble so much in your life you don't understand. Your brother's the victim. Get it? He's the victim, and the victim don't need a lawyer. The victim isn't supposed to keep quiet. The victim doesn't get any guarantees. I can stay here forever if I feel like it and ask as many questions as I want."

"Yeah? And what's to stop us from staying here forever and not answering any of them, huh? Tell me that, wise guy."

"Not a thing, Tullio, not a thing," Balzic said, reaching for his raincoat. "But there's one guarantee I will give you. I guarantee I'm going to keep asking until somebody gives me some answers. Your brother gets cut up, something is bent out of shape, and six will get you five it had something to do with somebody else's money. And I'll tell you something else, Tullio, and you better pay attention. Somebody else winds up in this hospital with so much as a split lip, I'm going to collar both of you. There isn't going to be any bullshit like that, you hear me? There hasn't been as long as I've been the man here, and it isn't going to start now. And just to make sure, I'm going to give the same message right now to Dom Muscotti, you hear me?"

"I hear you, Cheese, I hear you. What am I? Deaf? But I don't know what you're talking about."

"Oh you know all right. You know." Balzic pulled on his raincoat and walked out.

Balzic eased his cruiser out of the hospital parking lot and drove just fast enough to keep up with traffic, all the while trying to comprehend what had happened and why....

Armand Manditti had worked for years for Dom Muscotti as a runner. He picked up and delivered—money, betting slips, payoffs, layoffs, special case-lot orders of wine from state liquor stores for Dom, groceries and household necessities for Dom's mother—whatever Dom wanted or needed. Now, by Tullio's words, he was unemployed.

As for Tullio, he managed Muscotti's garbage dump. It was the third part of Muscotti's Rocksburg-bound empire. Since Muscotti's father before him, every piece of garbage collected in Rocksburg and in Bovard Township to the north, Westfield Township to the west, and Kennedy Township to the south and east—all public and private refuse—wound up on land owned by a Muscotti. It made no difference which collection outfit bid for the right to collect the stuff; they all paid Muscotti for the privilege of emptying their trucks. And long before anybody publicly talked about recycling waste, Dom's father and then Dom paid a squad of pickers, usually true wops—that is, Italians without papers—to swarm over each load as it was dumped and cull every tin, steel, or aluminum can they could find, then to separate, clean, and pulverize them into one-foot cubes to be sold wherever the market was best.

World War II guaranteed the family fortune in that third of Muscotti's empire; each load of garbage since only added to it, and the uproar over ecology did nothing in Rocksburg so much as show Muscotti the potential of paper and glass. Muscotti persuaded friends in Rocksburg's Sanitation Department who in turn prevailed upon Rocksburg's City Council to pass two ordinances: the first required that newspapers be bundled separately from other garbage; the second required that bottles and jars be placed in separate cans at each residence and business, public or private. While compliance with the two ordinances was far from total, it was sufficient to make life easier for Tullio's squad of pickers to turn garbage into money.

Garbage turned into money so fast that Muscotti had to start giving it away to keep from going into higher and higher tax brackets, and his philanthropy so charmed the Rocksburg Chamber of Commerce that in 1971 they named him Rocksburg's Man of the Year. It seemed not to matter to them that for fifteen years out of the last twenty Muscotti had been summoned to the Pittsburgh office of the Internal Revenue Service to explain his income, or that at least every other year for the past twenty-five Muscotti had been subpoenaed by county, state, and federal grand juries and assorted crime commissions to testify about the sources of his income. It also had not seemed to matter that Muscotti had been indicted six times, tried five times, and convicted three times since 1945 for operating lotteries and bookmaking establishments. What seemed to matter was his charity, though it had been rumored around town that the Chamber of Commerce was more concerned and greatly more relieved by the fact that there had been no violence even remotely attributable to Muscotti for sixteen years.

Bodies may have turned up in the trunks of cars in other parts of Conemaugh County, certain small newsstands and confectionaries in other towns may have suffered unexplained explosions, but nothing like that had happened in Rocksburg for sixteen years.

Balzic had to smile thinking about it. I been chief for sixteen years, he thought, and those Chamber guys never gave me a phone call. Maybe it was all just a coincidence....

Balzic parked his cruiser beside Muscotti's side door on State Street, and the smile left him. He was back to Armand Manditti again, Fat Manny who was alive only because of his fat, and to Tullio Manditti, who was behaving as though his brother was anything but a victim.

Balzic paused outside Muscotti's door and told himself that he had to control the anger he felt rising in him. There was no reason to believe that Manny's unemployment—if that were true—had anything at all to do with his being stabbed. Still, Balzic was getting a bad taste from fuming over that possibility, and he didn't want to blow the opportunity of finding out by losing his temper.

It was nearly five o'clock when Balzic came down the back stairs into Muscotti's. The bar was lined elbow to elbow with the mill and construction workers who habitually stopped after work to drink and learn the day's winning numbers. Shortly, the office brigade from the courthouse would be coming in, as would the merchants who kept shops in the vicinity. Some students from the county community college sat drinking beer out of quart bottles at one of the tables. At another sat Tom Murray, managing editor of *The Rocksburg Gazette*, with two of his reporters—Dick Dietz, who covered the courthouse, and Bob Armour, who covered City Hall. Surrounding the end of the bar nearest the side door were three of Muscotti's closest friends, Dom Scalzo, Tony DiLisi, and Bruno Cercone.

At the other end of the bar nearest the front door, Vinnie the bartender was arguing fruitlessly with Iron City Steve.

"If the war's over," Iron City Steve was shouting, his elbows flapping and his head bobbing, "how come we got all this combat?"

"Enough already!" Vinnie shouted back. "Just sit down and shut up a while. I had you up to my eyeballs today."

Steve's shoulder jerked and twitched. His hand sawed under his nose and then he pinched the corners of his mouth to wipe away beads of saliva. "You had enough, but who do I get enough of? I don't even see anybody I want a little piece of. . . ."

Balzic walked to that end of the bar, exchanging greetings with everyone he knew—which was everyone except for the students—and wondering why Dom Muscotti wasn't in sight.

"Are we approaching or proceeding?" Steve said to Balzic.

"Can't say for me, Steve. How 'bout you?"

"As for me, I approach a little, then I proceed a little. It all comes out the same—I don't go backward."

"Go sit down," Vinnie said. "Sit down and shut up or else go upstairs and go to sleep."

"See there?" Steve said, his hands flailing in all directions. "For every doer there's a teller. Comes out even that way. Gives everybody something to do."

"Shut up, I'm telling you. Jesus Christ, you been going since nine o'clock this morning."

"If I could just believe that," Steve said, picking up his beer and his muscatel and shuffling to the table nearest the front door.

"What'll it be, Mario?"

"Beer. Where's Dom?"

"He had to go someplace," Vinnie said, drawing the beer and setting it in front of Balzic. "He should be back pretty soon. What's the matter? You don't look too good."

"I don't feel too good right now, to tell you the truth. You hear about Fat Manny?"

"No. What about him?"

"Somebody tried to kill him."

Vinnie stopped wiping the bar, his face expressing genuine disbelief and surprise. "No shit. Who? What the hell for?"

"Pretty good questions. I thought maybe you might know something."

Hey, Mario, honest to God, this is the first I heard about it. When'd it happen?"

"Sometime this afternoon. Tullio came home from the dump and found him on the porch. Somebody really carved him up. Whoever it was wasn't fucking around."

"No-o shit. Man, oh man. Mario, I—I don't know what to say."

"What's the meeting about down the other end?"

"You mean Soup, Digs, and Brownie?" The names he used were the nicknames of Muscotti's friends.

Balzic nodded.

"Nothing special. Usual stuff, you know."

"Yeah? Well, do me a favor. Go down there and tell them what I just told you. I want to see what happens."

"Hey, Mario," Vinnie said, leaning close over the bar, "don't even talk like that. That ain't right."

"Just go tell them, will you please?"

"Okay, I'll tell them, but I'm telling you right now, Mario, you're thinking wrong. Those guys don't have nothing to do with Manny. Or Tullio either. If they got some bitch with either one of those two, I'd know about it, believe me. And they don't."

"I believe you. Just go tell them."

"Hey, Vinnie," someone called out. "Couple more here."

"Take it easy, take it easy. I only got two legs."

"Yeah? Well how 'bout using them?"

Vinnie shrugged at Balzic. "See what I got to listen to every day? Comedians. This should be Hollywood, and I should be Cecil B. DeMille. I got a cast of thousands in here every goddamn day." He hurried away to fill that order and then went to the far end of the bar, where he talked briefly with Scalzo, DiLisi, and Cercone.

Balzic couldn't see DiLisi's face too clearly, but Cercone looked like he was going to choke on his drink and Scalzo's face went slack. Scalzo shot a glance toward Balzic, then said something to the other two. He bent his head forward to hear their replies, then picked up his beer and came down the bar toward Balzic.

Scalzo, heavy-lidded, squatly built, indifferent about his appearance, and without pretensions about himself or his work, seemed more and more disturbed the nearer he came to Balzic. It figured, Balzic thought, that he would be the one to talk. He was much older than DiLisi or Cercone—he was sixty-four—and had been with Muscotti longer, since 1945, right after his discharge from the army. That had been his last legitimate employment and was the reason for his nickname. He had been a cook.

He set his beer on the bar and stood very close to Balzic. "What's this about Manny?"

"Well, it's this way, Soup. If it wasn't for all that grease on him, you'd be drinking to his memory."

"Now who the fuck'd want to do that? He's a pain in the ass,

Mario. You know that better than I do. But you got to admit, he never hurt nobody. He's just a slob, that's all."

"Well, he must've hurt somebody."

"Nah, I don't believe it. Somebody must've went nuts. Why? Why him? What do you think? You think something else?"

"Right now I'm not sure what I think. All I know is the same thing you know. He's been Dom's gofer for a lot of years, but in the hospital Tullio tells me he's unemployed."

Scalzo laughed. "Come on, you kiddin'? When wasn't he unemployed?"

"You know what I mean. Tullio says he don't work for anybody, though I got to admit he didn't say he wasn't working for Dom anymore exactly, but that was the impression I got—"

"Ah, Tullio's pulling your chain. He don't know what he's talking about. That was nothing. Dorn sets him down every once in a while. It's no big deal."

"Yeah, I know Dom's set him down occasionally before, and I got a pretty good idea why. But what was it for this time?"

Scalzo took a moment to reply. "Listen, Mario, I know you for a long time, right?"

Balzic nodded.

"Have I ever fucked around with the rules? Huh? Have I?"

"Not with me. No."

"Well, listen. Neither has Brownie and neither has Digs. I don't know what you're thinking, but I can see you're pissed off. But believe me, you got no right to even start thinking like, uh, well, you know, like sending Vinnie down there to tell us. Like you're going to watch us, you know? You shouldn't've done that, Mario. In fact, I'm a little surprised you did it."

"Well, maybe that was a little chicken-shit on my part, but it's been a long time since anything like this happened, and I'll be goddamned if it's going to get any bigger."

"Hey, I can see your point," Scalzo said. "I know what you mean. But me and Brownie and Digs got nothing to do with those two. They do whatever they do for Dom. We don't have nothing to do with them, believe me. I don't like Tullio. Never did. I used to go up their house when their old man was alive. I liked the old guy. We used to sit around and drink his wine and play *morra*. Even then I didn't like Tullio. He was always a smartmouth. Even when he's three, four years old, he was a wise little prick. And all the trouble Manny got in, all the trouble he ever got in, it was 'cause Tullio put him up to it. And Manny always got caught. See, Manny ain't too swift in the head, and the old man used to look out for him, and Tullio, he didn't like it. So he was always trying to get Manny in the heat with the old man. It's the same way now. They're the same way with Dom. Tullio tells him, 'Hey, don't turn all them numbers in. Who's going to know?' Shit like that. But Manny always fucks up somehow, you know."

"Is that what happened this time?" Balzic said.

Scalzo shrugged. "Hey, maybe I said too much already. I think maybe you better ask Dom. I'll tell you what. Ask Vinnie. He knows more about that than I do. Believe me." Scalzo picked up his beer and took a sip. "Mario, I been around a long time. Believe me, don't try to make nothing out of this. Somebody went nuts. Had to. Couldn't be nothing else."

Balzic shrugged. "Well, I'll tell you this, Soup. I'm going to keep asking until I find out you're right, how's that? And believe me, I hope you are right."

"I'm right. You'll see," Scalzo said, turning away and walking back down the bar to where Cercone and DiLisi were waiting for him.

Balzic stared moodily at his beer, then picked it up and drained the glass in four swallows, holding it up when he finished for Vinnie to refill it.

Vinnie refilled his glass and set it on the bar. He took some moments wiping the bar and the stem of the glass. "So what'd they say?"

"Soup says they don't know anything about Manny or Tullio."

"Ain't that what I said? Huh?"

Balzic nodded. "He also said to ask you. He said you knew more about those two than he did. Or Digs or Brownie."

"I already told you, Mario. They couldn't have any bitch with those two fat-asses or I'd know about it. Ain't that what I said?"

"That's what you said, all right. So tell me. Is Manny still running for Dom? Tullio says he isn't."

"Listen, Mario, I could tell you, but I think it's better you hear it from Dom, you know?"

"So he isn't."

Vinnie nodded with his eyes downcast and then shrugged. "I don't think it's any different this time than it was all those other times, understand. But you talk to Dom. I got enough aggravation with him lately. He even thinks I'm putting any more of his business in the street, I won't be able to live with him—which ain't to say I been putting any of his business in the street. But he thinks I have."

"What's your aggravation with him?"

"Oh, Mario, honest to God, you don't know?"

"I don't know what you're talking about."

Vinnie nodded for them to move to the very end of the bar. He faced the window overlooking Main Street and spoke very softly. Balzic had to lean over the bar to hear him.

"How old is he?" Vinnie began. "Fifty-seven, right?"

Balzic nodded and shrugged.

"You know how long since he could get it up? Five years. All that Canadian Club. Why do you think I quit drinking? I take maybe two shots of brandy a day. One in my coffee, the other one around noon. He told me to quit. *He* told *me*, get it? So what do you think now?"

"Oh don't tell me."

"Yeah. Younger than his daughters for crissake."

"Hey, it happens, Vinnie. It happens. It's happened to better men than him."

"Hey, those better men ain't got his wife. She ever finds out for sure, I'm going to be the second one she buries."

"You mean she asked you?"

Vinnie shook his head and winced. "She called me at home last week. You know the last time she called me? When Dom's father died. Twenty-two fucking years ago, that's the last time she called me at home. You know what she asks me? She wants to know how's business. How's business! Are you kiddin'? You should've heard the lies I told her. Jesus Christ, I should get an Oscar for that performance."

"What's wrong? How's she know something's up?"

"The register's down a yard, a yard and a half every week for like two months now." Vinnie shook his head and sighed. "This fucking Tuscan, what is he? A medical miracle? He got to get a hard-on now? And me, I'm in the middle. I got to be nice to the broad, you know. Whatever she wants. Booze, bread, food—oh, Christ. I'll tell you, Mario, I wasn't this scared when Sammy Weisberg was still alive. Dom's old lady is something else. Ah, what am I telling you for?"

"Is he dipping into the other stuff or just the register for her?"

"What do you think? I'm telling you, I'm ready to go to California or some fucking place. This has got me nuts. And him, he's like in junior high school, the way he's acting. Twenty, thirty beans every day. Oh, brother. You know what really scares me? Sometimes I think the bastard really wants to hear how big the bang's going to be."

"It'll make some noise all right."

"Hey, Vinnie, you working today or not?" someone called out down the bar.

"Keep your pants on, what is this?" Vinnie shouted back. He started to hustle away but came back. "You know what I did last Sunday? Go ahead, think about it."

"I can guess."

"Uh-huh. First time since I buried my mother. On my knees, with a candle, in front of Mary yet. Holy fucking Christ. . . ."

Balzic shook his head sympathetically and then resumed staring at his beer between sips. He drank that one and another before he heard the door open behind him and heard Dom Muscotti's voice speaking in Italian to someone still on the sidewalk.

The first person Muscotti saw after he closed the door was Balzic, and he smiled broadly and extended his hand, asking in Italian how Balzic was.

"I'll know better after we talk."

"In the back?"

"In the back."

Muscotti had held Balzic's hand until then. It was a strong grip but with no attempt to show strength, for Muscotti, in spite of his age and perpetual drinking, was somehow still a powerful man. Except that his once-red hair was now iron gray, the only obvious signs of aging about him were the deepening creases in his face and neck and the increasing paunch below his belt. He had given up driving an automobile years ago, and no matter what the temperature or the weather, he walked everywhere without an outer coat. He would ride in an automobile only when he had to leave Rocksburg, asking for a lift from whoever happened to be in his saloon and paying for it with drinks. His shoes were handmade in Philadelphia, and he joked that he would live only about a year longer than his shoemaker.

Speaking to everyone by name, Muscotti led Balzic to the second of two small rooms beyond the kitchen. He held the door for Balzic, flipped the switch for the light over the round table in the center of the room, then closed and locked the door behind them. There were ten chairs in the room, seven of them around the table, and two ancient, wooden filing cabinets in one corner. Muscotti went to the nearest of those and brought out a bottle of Valpolicella and two thick-stemmed glasses.

"Sit, Mario, sit," Muscotti said, screwing out the cork and pouring the wine to within a half-inch of the tops of the glasses.

Balzic picked up one of the glasses and toasted Muscotti's health while still standing. Muscotti returned the toast and then they both sat, pulling out the chairs and sitting obliquely facing each other.

"How's your mother, Mario?"

"Fine. How's yours?"

"Oh, couldn't be better. She's a little mad at me though."

"Why's that?"

"I made her put her money in the bank. She says to me, 'All of it?' And I said, 'Well, you can keep a little in the house.' So how much you think she wants to keep?"

"How much?"

"Five grand. 'Just in case,' she says. Can you beat that? I said to her, 'Hey, what kind of emergency you think you're going to have?' She just laughed. I laughed like hell myself." Muscotti drank the rest of his wine and said, "Drink up, Mario. Have some more."

"Thank you," Balzic said, drinking his and then watching the color of the wine as Muscotti refilled the glasses.

"How's Ruth? Emily, Marie—they okay?"

"They're fine," Balzic said. "Your family?"

"Oh, you know. What do they got to complain about? Hey,

did I tell you what I got my daughters for last Christmas? I think I must've told everybody but you."

Balzic shook his head.

"Telephone credit cards. They're better than all the rest of those cards. You can get anything on those AT&T cards, d'you know that? I told them, I said, 'Hey, don't you do it. Just phone calls, that's all,'" Muscotti said, laughing. "Those credit cards, Christ, what a friggin' hustle. I wish I'd've thought of them. They're better than football. Better than boxing used to be."

Balzic coughed and crossed and uncrossed his legs.

Muscotti had been sitting back in his chair. Now he straightened up and put his hands on his knees, looking directly into Balzic's eyes. "Okay, Mario, I'm listening."

"You know about Fat Manny?"

Muscotti nodded. "I heard right before I came in. Young DeNezza told me out on the street."

"Well, what's going on?"

"I don't know," Muscotti said, shrugging.

"Is he still running for you?"

"No."

"Why not? What happened?"

"He did something he wasn't supposed to do."

"Hey, listen, Dom, maybe you don't see what I see—"

"Oh, Mario, wait a minute. I see plenty. I knew you were going to be here as soon as young DeNezza told me. I said to myself, I'll bet a hundred to one Mario's waiting for me when I get inside."

"Okay, so you won. So what's going on?"

"Mario, I'm telling you, I don't know."

"But for sure he's not working for you anymore."

"Oh, you know, it wasn't nothing permanent. I just had to sit him down a little while, that's all. He'd've got his job back."

Balzic sipped his wine and thought a moment. "Dom, sixteen years ago next month, we made some rules, remember?"

"I remember," Muscotti said, nodding vigorously.

"No whores, no dope, no muscle, right?"

"That's right."

"And it never cost you a penny tax, right?"

"Not to you, that's right."

"Or to any of my people either."

"I can't argue with that."

"So all of a sudden we get some muscle and you're telling me you don't know anything about it?"

"Mario, honest to God, I don't. It shocked me to hear it. I mean it. I don't know where it came from or why. On my father's grave it didn't come from me. What the hell do I want with muscle? What am I—one of those crazy New York guys? All muscle does is bring heat. Who the hell wants heat? Right now, look what's happening. Somebody goes Hollywood, and here you are, looking at me like I'm a crazy. Christ, Mario, how long's it been since we talked back here like this? You think I want this?" Muscotti threw up his hands. "Over Fat Manny?"

"Okay," Balzic said. "So why'd you sit him down? Was he booking on his own?"

"What do you think?"

"I'm asking. Was he?"

"Yeah, sure. What else? The sonofabitch, I should've had him out the dump. That was my mistake. Giving him something better because my mother likes him. I should've put him out there."

"Why didn't you?"

"I just told you. My mother likes him. He brings the groceries, they sit around and gossip. He knows just what to tell her. She feeds him, he eats like six plates of pasta, he tells her how she's the best cook in the world since his mother died, and she loves him. Then he tells her who he saw coming out of church, who was in the A&P, who was buying zucchini, who was buying eggplant, and she wants to know all that stuff. I tried other guys. They don't know how to talk to her. She gets mad and I got to put him back on. She's really been hollering at me since I set him down this time."

"How long's it been this time?"

"A week."

"Okay, so he booked something and he got beat. You don't think there could be any other reason?"

"What else? He books a winner, he can't pay, the guy takes the heat. What the fuck—I'd do the same thing myself." Dom shook his head. "I told the goddamn dummy a hundred times. I said, 'Manny, you can't do this. One of these times you're going to get burned, and everybody's going to think I'm backing you. And I ain't. And you're going to have to take the weight, and where the fuck are you going to get the five-forty if you take a buck on a solid hit? You ain't getting it from me; not even at five percent a week, you ain't getting it.' I told him that so many times I can't count them. You think he listens? Huh? What am I talking for?

"What kills me, you know when he does it? Five minutes after he passes a bakery. He sees all those jelly doughnuts and cream puffs in the window and right away the eraser starts going. He got twenty, twenty-two bets, he turns in eighteen. And that friggin' Tullio, he tells Manny, 'Don't worry about it. Dom got so much paper the government's coming to him. What's a buck and a half to Dom?' And friggin' Manny listens to him and thinks it's all right. I'd like to kick Tullio's ass myself. Manny's too. But see, Manny ain't as smart as Tullio. So as mad as I get at him, I really can't get too mad, you know? 'Cause he's dumb ...

I should've kicked his ass the first time he did it. I knew this was going to happen...."

"Well, you kick both their asses if you want to, but there's two things you better do first."

"Me? What do you want me to do?"

"First, tell Tullio not to get any ideas. 'Cause something happens, I'm going to come straight to you."

"Aw, Mario—"

"Aw Mario nothing. We made the rules. You and me. You get the action, you keep the odds right, you pay no taxes. Everybody who wins gets paid, and no more than five percent on the shylocking to the losers. Did I leave anything out?"

"No."

"Okay. Then convince Tullio."

"Or else?"

"Or else you all go to the slam, and I'll fix it so everybody has to put up cash bonds. All the street people you got. It'll cost you a fortune."

"But, Mario, you know it's not me!"

"I know it's not. But I'm making it you. Because Tullio won't listen to me. He thinks I'm a jackoff. *Your* jackoff. But he does something, and everything stops. And it won't be me serving the warrants. It'll be U.S. marshalls."

"Aw, come on now, Mario. I been straight with you all these years and you're going to talk like this to me? Over something you know I didn't have nothing to do with?"

"All I'm telling you to do is tell Tullio. Because, Dom, this town is not going back to the way things were when Collela was chief and you and Sammy Weisberg were burning each other down. Collela worked both of you pretty good, and from what I heard he paid seventy-five thousand for that place in Florida. Which must've made you and Weisberg feel pretty smart."

Balzic stabbed the air with his index finger. "Goddamnit, I don't have any retirement like that to look forward to, and you got a lot more money because I don't. So you tell Tullio."

"Okay, Mario, okay, take it easy," Muscotti said, shaking his head with his eyes downcast. "But I can't make any miracle for you. Some things you just can't control."

"Put somebody on him."

"Like who?"

"Cercone would make a good keeper. Tell him what's going to happen."

"Brownie? At the dump?"

"Hey, Dom, how you handle it is how you handle it. All I'll tell you is this: I'll do everything I can to find whoever it was as fast as I can. Which brings up the second thing you have to do. Tell Manny to quit listening to Tullio. As long as Tullio's got his ear, Manny's not going to tell me anything. But he opens up, it's simple. I go collar the guy and that's that. But if Manny keeps shut, then I got to find the guy myself, which is going to take time, which is going to give Tullio time, which means you got to keep somebody on him longer, which means you lose business somewhere else. And if Tullio shakes whoever you put on him and does something stupid, then I guarantee it'll cost you a fortune in bail."

Muscotti shook his head and rubbed his palms together. "That fat-ass. I should've got him on with the county. Dumb as he is, he ought to be working for the government."

Balzic drove immediately to his station after leaving Muscotti's. He was so preoccupied with what he'd said to Muscotti and the way he'd said it that he ran a red light two blocks from City Hall, spinning the wheel wildly to swerve between a pickup truck and a station wagon loaded with cub scouts. He didn't even slow down. He slouched against the seat, tucking his chin into the lapels of his raincoat, and hoped he hadn't been recognized.

Going up the steps, he said under his breath, "You dumb bastard, it's a good thing you got sense enough to have an unmarked car...."

Inside the duty room he found Desk Sergeant Vic Stramsky talking on the phone, taking a description.

"Another runaway," Stramsky said after hanging up. "Cleaned out his old lady's purse and split. Thirteen years old. I wonder how far he thinks he's going to get on four bucks and change."

"Well, put it out to the troops," Balzic said. "Maybe we'll get lucky with this one. What's that, the third one this week?"

"Yeah," Stramsky said, nodding, "but we found the second one."

"Well, that makes it two to one, the kids are still leading." Balzic went to the coffee urn and poured himself a cup. He took a sip and scalded his lips, spitting the coffee on the floor. "What the hell's wrong with this machine? Everything comes out boiling."

Stramsky ignored him, rolling over to the radio console and putting out the name and description of the runaway. When he was finished, he said, "What're you screaming at the machine for? If you know everything's coming out boiling, why can't you wait?"

"Go ahead, give me a lecture about patience. My head's going six ways at once—all wrong—and I'm supposed to improve my character. I burn myself once more, that machine goes in the can, and nobody'll have to worry about my character." He went to the log on the table in front of the radio console and ran his finger down the list of calls. "Some day this is. Two bent fenders, a mattress fire, a runaway, and Fat Manny—and he doesn't even make the log."

A FIX LIKE THIS

"What're you mumbling about?" Stramsky said, rolling his chair over beside Balzic.

"Put down here that Armand Manditti was the victim of felonious assault, sometime between three-thirty and four-thirty. Assailant unknown. Give it the whole treatment."

"Did you say Fat Manny?"

"Yeah. Listen, I'm going up to Norwood."

"Why?"

"Because that's where Manny got it."

Stramsky started to smile, but caught himself and turned away.

"What's so funny?"

"You. You're really gunned up about something. If you were going up to Norwood, why'd you come back here? You could've told me that on the radio."

Balzic snorted. "You think that's pretty dumb, huh?"

"Well, you know...."

"Yeah? Well, you should've seen me ducking after I almost took the front end off a station wagon full of kids. You'd've really got your jollies over that.... What the hell do I know what I came back for? Maybe to burn my mouth on the coffee, all the weight I tried to lay on Muscotti. I couldn't believe it was me talking."

Stramsky chortled. "What'd you say to him?"

Before Balzic could reply, the phone rang. Stramsky answered it and then held it out for Balzic. "It's Johnson from the state CID."

"Hello, Walk. What do you got?"

"Not much, buddy. But I'll tell you one thing. You weren't joking about those two being slobs. I never saw a house like that. God, newspapers up to the ceiling in, uh, I guess it was the living room; garbage in the kitchen you wouldn't believe; in the bathroom, so help me, there was a radiator and two batteries for a car. And stink! Jesus. You couldn't tell if there had been a struggle or not. My people kept looking at me and saying, 'How would we know?'"

"Yeah. So did you get anything?"

"We scraped up a lot of blood. There was no forcible entry. We got a couple sets of prints, but that's really the best I can offer."

"How about somebody stepping in the blood—any chance?"

"No. There was a lot of stepping and stumbling going on, but not one damn thing clear."

"How about tire tracks?"

"All over the place, but we could only make out one matched set, and then when this Tullio showed up, it didn't take any expert to see they were all off his car." Johnson paused and chuckled. "That Tullio, is he something. He came in and started screaming where was our search warrant. I tried to tell him that his brother was the victim and that his residence was the scene of a crime, but I wasted my breath. He raised holy hell for about ten minutes, then all of a sudden he says, 'I got to take a bath. Don't bother me no more.' And off he goes and takes a bath."

"So, uh, you really didn't get anything, huh?"

"Sorry, Mario. I wish I could give you something more, but about the only thing I have are the prints. I sent our print man up to the hospital to get the victim's, and we got Tullio's. Once we get a comparison we might have something, but that's about it."

"Well, thanks, Walk, I appreciate it."

"Listen, you also weren't kidding about the neighbors. I didn't find one who could speak English."

"Oh, they can all right, don't kid yourself. But they won't. Not even to me." Balzic sighed. "Okay, Walk. So let me know how the prints turn out."

"Will do. Take it easy."

Balzic hung up and swore.

"I take it they didn't come up with anything," Stramsky said.

"You take it right, brother."

"So now tell me what you said to Muscotti."

"Huh? Oh. Nothing much. I just told him that if anything happens because of Manny getting chopped up, I was going to guarantee his whole operation was going to the slammer, that's all. Just the goddamnedest threat I ever made in my life. And then I sat there with all the face in the world and tried to make out like it's no threat. Like it's a sure pop. Christ, I must be watching too much television or something. But you know the real capper?"

Stramsky shook his head.

"I think he bought it, how's that grab you?" Balzic shook his head and snorted softly. "Now can you feature me walking into the U.S. Attorney's office in Pittsburgh, bigger than shit, and I'm trying to convince those guys that I let the second biggest banker and lay-offer in the county—I let him run for sixteen years, and not only did I never bust him or anybody connected with him, but I never took a penny from him. Now just what do you think they're going to say? They're not going to be able to say anything. They'll all be laughing so hard they'll have hernias."

"Don't you think Dom knows that? Or don't you think he's going to think of it?"

"I don't know. The look on his face, I couldn't believe it. But maybe all that Canadian Club finally got to his brain. Then again, maybe he got himself in too deep in something else."

"What's that?"

"Something Vinnie told me. Seems that old Tuscan is going to do adolescence over again. He got Vinnie so shook up, Vinnie went to church last Sunday and put up a candle in front of Mary. Dom's wife finds out for sure what's going on, everybody'll be putting up candles in front of St. Jude."

"You mean Dom got himself a broad?" Stramsky threw back his head and roared with laughter.

"Yeah, it's funny now, but what do you think's going to happen when his old lady starts asking him how come the register's down a yard and a half every week? How many stories you think he can come up with?"

"Is that what he's throwing at the broad?"

"According to Vinnie. I'll tell you, I never saw Vinnie so rattled. Which, the more I think about it, the more I think is the reason Dom bought my bullshit." Balzic sighed heavily. "Which just gives me another thought. Holy Christ!"

"What's the matter?"

"The matter is, Dom's old lady blows the whistle on him, we're right back in the U.S. Attorney's office, are you kidding?"

"So? You're clean. The whole force is clean."

"Come on, Vic, you know better than that. There's two ways to be dirty. Everybody knows the first way. The second applies to us. We don't do what we get paid to do, we're dirty, brother, and that is all she wrote."

"Hey, Mario, don't you think you're getting a little carried away? Hell, Dom's wife never goes near his joint. And who's going to tell her?"

"Nobody has to, Vic. She's already wise. She called Vinnie at home last week and asked him how business was. She knows something's up. She goes through Dom's pants every night as soon as he starts snoring. Hell, Dom'll tell you that himself. She just hasn't figured out how come he's been short—oh, Jesus Christ." Balzic clapped his hands and threw them upward and then held his head. "No wonder he bought it! He's looking at me and listening to me, but he's hearing his old lady."

"I don't get it," Stramsky said.

"Dom. I'm thinking he bought *my* bullshit. But that's exactly the same story his wife's going to give him. The only difference is I was bitching about Manny. But he's already been through this in his head with his wife. In his head, he knows that's what she's going to say. I could've been talking about the broad for all the difference it makes. He knew goddamn well I can't put him in the slammer without taking a lot of heat myself, but she can put him away forever just on the income taxes alone. Ho, boy, what an ego I got. I wish I had a brain to match." Balzic pounded his fist on a desk and then walked quickly toward the door.

"Hey, where you going now?"

"Someplace. Wherever I can find somebody smarter than me. Wherever the hell that is. Hell, right now that's practically anyplace."

Balzic took the alleys to avoid traffic, pulling in ten minutes later to the rear parking lot of Rocksburg Bowl. He hustled inside to the lounge and bar, looking around for Mo Valcanas. It had to be ladies' day at the bowling alleys because the only man Balzic saw was the bartender, an aging and overweight one-time pretty boy who brushed his hair with his hands and straightened his tie each time he filled an order. He seemed to have found paradise serving alcohol and stale jokes to leagues of women bowlers. Balzic surmised this in a minute, then started for the room behind the bar where the gin games were played daily.

He found only Mo Valcanas and Dick Gervasi, the owner of the alleys, playing cards. Gervasi was writing on a small pad, and Valcanas was shuffling the cards while trying to read the score upside down. Both looked up at the same time.

"Mario," Gervasi said. "Long time no see, buddy. Where you been keeping yourself?"

"It should be longer," Valcanas said. "He comes here, he's got something in mind for me."

"Gentlemen," Balzic said, drawing up a chair and straddling it. "I'll come right to the point."

"The day any cop comes right to the point will be a first in American history," Valcanas said. "And that includes you."

"Oh, you're so sweet. I could just give you a big kiss."

"You want something to drink, Mario?" Gervasi said, standing.

"No, thanks. What I really want is to talk to the Greek for a couple minutes. You mind?"

"What the hell are you asking him for? You want to talk to me, why don't you ask me if I mind?"

"Oh, you're so lovable. I'll bet your mother just beamed the whole nine months, just beamed and glowed waiting for you to pop your cute little bald head out."

"Hey, I'll be glad to let you two alone, Mario. This Greek's killing me today. I need a breather."

"I see you got a new bartender," Balzic said. "What happened to Jimmy?"

"He's in the hospital. He'll be back in a couple weeks. You sure you don't want something to drink?" Gervasi went for the door.

"Nah. I had plenty already today."

Gervasi left then, closing the door firmly behind him.

"Okay, Mario," Valcanas said, "I hesitate to ask, but what is it this time?"

"Just a couple questions about the law, that's all."

"And naturally these couple answers I'm expected to give will be for free. You couldn't ask in my office, where I might feel justified in sending you a bill."

"Naturally. Besides, every time I walk into your office I start to feel like I'm really in trouble, like I really need a lawyer."

"Uh-huh," Valcanas grumbled. "I ought to set up an office in all the saloons I go into. I might start making some money."

"Boy, there's a contradiction for you. You set up offices in all the saloons you go into, you Couldn't afford the light bills."

"Well, let's quit fucking around. It'll cost you two drinks. I got to get that much out of you."

"Fair enough. So here it is: now I know that a wife can't be forced to testify against her husband, but how about if she volunteers? What's she worth on the stand?"

"That depends. Give me a situation."

"Well, the woman, after a long and faithful marriage on her part, finds out that her old man's screwing around, which he's never done before. In the meantime, he's been involved for most of his adult life in illegal activities. She may not be an accomplice exactly, but she's the closest thing to it there is. She knows everything, in other words."

Valcanas grinned and then broke up laughing. "Christ, don't tell me you're getting worried about Dom too? Half the goddamn courthouse is walking around on eggs about that. That's all I've heard down there for the past two weeks."

"Well, I guess I must be the dumbest guy in town then."

"You said it, Mario, I didn't."

"Aw fuck you too. Well, what about it? How much damage can she do?"

"That would depend on a couple of things. First, it would depend on whether she has access to records or had been keeping records herself. I mean, her credibility goes down to practically zero if she just walks into the U.S. Attorney's office and says, 'I know my husband did this or that or whatever.' That's for openers. Then suppose she has records, enough to get the whole thing to trial. It would depend on the attorneys—how good the prosecutor was in leading her through her motivation for coming forward at this late date in her life—and on his lawyer—Dom's—for trying to wreck that motivation. But the big thing would be the jury. The prosecution would want as many old ladies in the jury box as they could get, preferably Italian Catholic, and the defense would want as many dirty old men as they could get. Whoever wins that battle wins the war, that's what it comes down to."

"So given the worst suppositions, Dom's wife could really raise some hell."

"If you have something to be concerned about, sure. Hell, Corcoran is so rattled that yesterday he called a recess in the middle of a drunk-driving trial. Two more minutes and it would've been over. But he called a recess. I thought his tipstaff was going to faint. But, hell, Corcoran's got reason to be nervous. All the fines he's laid on Dom's people in the last eight years wouldn't add up to two thousand bucks. That time the state boy scouts caught Digs DiLisi with forty-two-thousand bucks and about ten pounds of numbers slips, Corcoran let him off with costs. Just what do you think that was worth?"

"I don't even want to guess," Balzic said.

"Well, you ever get curious, you go ask Digs how much was in the briefcase when he went to pick it up. He came bitching to me afterward, and I told him, I said, 'You dumb bastard, you ought to be glad you got that much back. Maybe now you'll think of something better to do with those slips than leave them laying around on your kitchen table.'"

"But I thought you beat that for him."

Valcanas smiled. "Come on. I filed a motion to suppress evidence on the grounds that the boy scouts' information was based on hearsay. The law's changed now, you know that. Now the so-called confidential informant has to appear himself in front of the magistrate. But then, Christ, a cop's hearsay was good enough.

"Anyway," Valcanas went on, "if I hadn't known that

Corcoran was going to hear the damned thing, I wouldn't even have wasted my secretary's time typing up the motion to suppress. But I knew what he'd do. Exactly what he did, which was give Digs a speech about how the tentacles of gambling reach into all sorts of nasty nasties, and then fine him a hundred bucks and costs. But Digs, that egotistical ass, he can't get it through his head that you put forty-two big ones on the wheel of justice, somebody pushing is going to think lifting is easier. And to this day, he thinks that if it had come up in front of some of Dom's other friends, my motion to suppress—to put it mildly—would've been received with anything more than a smile. He thinks those other guys would've hit him with a fine and costs—and let him walk out with a full briefcase.

"Christ, sometimes these wops make me laugh. He gets half a briefcase back, and he gets pissed at me. He says—and I quote—'It would've been cheaper to go to jail.' I said, 'Why you stupid sonofabitch, you go to jail and you don't get anything back.' But do you know, to this day he's never paid my bill. Not only that, he refuses to speak to me. Christ...."

Balzic chewed his thumbnail thoughtfully.

"Besides which," Valcanas said, shifting around on his chair, "this has got to be the biggest joke in this county since Froggy ran for judge."

"Why's that?"

"Dom's not screwing anybody for crissake. He can't. You can't drink as much as he drinks and still grind your organ. If anything, his genitourinary tract is in worse shape than mine—if that's possible."

"Well, I wouldn't pretend to know whether he's screwing anybody," Balzic said. "But a hell of a lot of people seem to think so. And his wife know's the register's short in his saloon. What difference does it make whether he is or isn't or can or can't—if she thinks he is, what's the difference?"

"None. If she acts on what she thinks. If that is what she thinks. Why don't you ask her and be a real cop—prevent a crime instead of waiting until it happens and then trying to prove that whoever you caught is the person who did it? Hell, what could be more salutary than that?"

"Oh, up yours. What do I say? 'Hey, Gina, there's something I been meaning to ask you—is that how I start?"

"How you ask is your problem. I'm not interested in the answer myself. All I know is, the most Dom can do is rub bellies. And that would be pure nostalgia. I'll make you a bet though."

"What bet?"

"I'll lay twenty against one that all he's doing with that broad—whoever she is—is talking. And giving her money for being kind enough to listen. People are waiting in line to talk to the brain strainers, either because it's fashionable or because their families can't stand them anymore. But can you feature Dom going to a shrink? Hell, I can imagine him exposing himself to a little girl sooner than I can see him admitting that there was something going on in his head he couldn't handle.

"And what about a priest?" Valcanas went on. "You know what a priest is to Dom? He's a guy in funny clothes who read too many books when he was a kid because the nuns scared the shit out of him. And all he's good for is saying the words that make your wife feel all right about screwing you, or that make the family feel okay when somebody dies. But most of all, he's good for saying the right words in front of a jury when you get busted for running a book. And unless he's had some genuine change of mind, those are the reasons he takes up the collection every Sunday at twelve o'clock mass. Go ask Marrazo if I'm not right. Better yet, go ask him if Dom ever came to him with a problem—any problem."

"I don't have to ask," Balzic said. "Most of what you said I agree with, except for that part about paying the broad just to listen."

"Oh, come on, Mario. Hell, I had a client once who used to pay a whore fifty bucks an hour once a week, sometimes twice, just so he could cuss her out and call her names. He never went within three feet of her. What do you think he was doing?"

"You tell me."

"He was telling her everything he didn't have the guts to tell his wife. The whore used to sit around doing her nails, listening to records, and all she was required to do was look up every ten minutes or so and say, 'What do you know about it, dummy?' Then he was off for another ten minutes. But do you think his wife believed that? Especially after she went to the trouble of hiring a private dick to find out where he was going? And you want to hear something really stupid? I actually arranged a meeting in my office."

"Oh, are you kiddin' me?" Balzic said, laughing. "With the wife and the whore?"

Valcanas scratched his throat slowly. "I was a lot younger then. A lot younger. God, when I think about it, I can't believe I was ever that young."

When Balzic finally quit laughing, he said, "I still can't get it through my head. I—"

"Look," Valcanas said, "I know you talk with Marrazo a lot. And I think I know you well enough to be reasonably sure that if something was really bothering you, you'd go to a shrink. But what do you think would happen in this town if word got around that the chief of police was seeing a shrink?"

"I wouldn't tell anybody about it."

"Then what's so hard to understand about paying a broad to listen to you?"

"I don't understand it because I can't see myself doing it, that's all."

"Well, Christ, you just said that if you had to go to a shrink you wouldn't tell anybody about it. Now you say you can't see yourself paying a broad for practically the same thing. You're as bad as the people you'd be scared of."

"That's not what I mean."

"Oh, hell, I'm starting to get thirsty. You owe me two drinks, don't forget."

"I didn't forget."

"Then let's go get them," Valcanas said, standing and going toward the door. He stopped short of it. "Think about this, Mario. You wouldn't tell anybody about going to a shrink; now just try to imagine what happens to the *padrone*. I mean, who's he have to talk to? Don't forget, you and I both know where Dom fits in the scheme of things in this part of the state, but most people around here have a vastly inflated notion of who he is and what he can do. And the ones who work for him? Christ, they think he's got a bulletproof soul, except for Vinnie. Vinnie knows that's a crock. He knows Dom better than anybody."

"Well, okay," Balzic said, "but just for the sake of argument, if he does need somebody to talk to, why wouldn't he go to his *padrone?*"

"How should I know? I don't know their rules. For all I know they may play as many silly word games as the Shriners. Maybe there are some things they just don't talk about. Hell, I don't know what's ailing Dom—if anything is. Maybe he suddenly found out he's mortal. Maybe he started paying attention in church. I don't know. Go talk to the broad, I'm telling you. Find out what she's like. See what her angle is. Or go talk to Marrazo. Maybe he knows something. But if you really want to know what's going on, talk to the broad. That's what I'd do . . . come on. You owe me two drinks."

They went out to the bar and Balzic ordered for Valcanas.

"Don't you want anything?" Valcanas asked.

"No. I'm trying to think where I should go, whether I should go talk to the broad or to Father Marrazo."

"You know, Mario," Valcanas said after his drink came, "I'm starting to wonder why you're so concerned about this in the first place."

Balzic shrugged. "Something happened today that is really giving off a bad odor. If I don't get it straightened out in a hurry, it might stink all the way to Pittsburgh. And believe me, the last thing I want is for that U.S. Attorney to get his nose open—no matter what causes it to get open . . . I'll see you, Mo. Try not to hurt anybody driving home."

"Aw go pound sand. Hey, what about the other drink?"

"I owe you one," Balzic said, laughing and clapping Valcanas lightly on the shoulder as he turned to leave. He heard Valcanas cursing in Greek as he left.

Balzic went in the back door of St. Malachy's rectory. He found the door to Father Marrazo's study slightly ajar and knocked gently. He heard some movement but no answer to his knock, so he pushed the door a bit more open.

The priest was sitting at his desk as though he had just put something on the floor, and when he saw that it was Balzic he reached down and brought up a jelly glass half full of wine and an unlabeled bottle which looked to be about two-thirds empty. He didn't bother to stand or speak, nor did he smile. He simply looked at Balzic and then nodded toward a chair for Balzic to sit. He opened a drawer in his desk and brought out another jelly glass, filling it and his own, again nodding to Balzic to have the wine.

"*Salud,*" the priest said, just above a whisper. He drank half his glass without waiting for Balzic to return the toast.

Balzic sipped the wine, just enough to taste it, then put the glass back on the desk and sat in the chair the priest had nodded to.

"Uh, Father, you sick?"

"Not physically, no."

"Well, uh, listen, if there's a better time for me to come back, you know, just say the word and I'll—"

"No, no. Don't leave. Let's just drink some wine and sit here a little while."

Balzic waited some moments, sipping the wine. Then he asked, "Is it that bad?"

"Mario, it's the worst thing—ah, listen to me. I almost said it's the worst thing that's happened to me since I've been in this parish, but that's how bad it is. It's got me thinking about myself instead of what's really involved, as though—ah, never mind . . . I'm really glad you came. There's nobody I know better able to understand this . . . but, please. Drink up."

Balzic took up his glass and drank. "Is this Mr. Ferrarra's wine?"

The priest nodded. "And when we finish this, I've got another bottle, and if we finish that—if you're still here —I've got a half-gallon of California chablis." The priest spoke with his eyes closed, and his face was going through the very obvious contortions of a man trying to keep from crying.

Balzic lit a cigarette and sat on the edge of his chair, trying to decide whether to speak or keep silent. He couldn't recall ever seeing the priest so distraught.

Some minutes passed. They emptied their glasses, the priest refilled them, and they drank that. The bottle was almost empty. Father Marrazo looked at it, poured the last drops into Balzic's glass, and then left the room. He reappeared shortly, carrying another bottle of Mr. Ferrarra's homemade wine in one hand and the chablis in the other. He set both bottles on his desk and refilled their glasses from the Ferrarra. Then he sank slowly into his chair, picking up his glass and holding it up to the light. "What a color," he said. "Isn't it beautiful?"

"Lovely."

". . . he taught my introductory course in philosophy, can you imagine? Good Lord, how long ago was that?"

Balzic frowned quizzically but said nothing.

"What a roar he caused over at St. Vincent's," Father Marrazo said. "He was supposed to be giving us Aristotle and Augustine and Aquinas, and there he was, throwing Kierkegaard and Heidegger and Jaspers at us as well. My God, it's a wonder he was allowed to go on as long as he did. But, uh, he left eventually. In my junior year. He was made assistant here, and then when he got to be too much here, out he went to St. Jude's."

"Uh, Father, who're you talking about?"

"What? Oh, I'm sorry, Mario. I thought I said. Father Sabatine. From St. Jude's, out in Westfield Township."

"I think I might've met him," Balzic said, "but I don't know him."

"Oh, he raised some hell in this diocese, believe me. He had old ladies of both sexes running to the bishop every week about something he said the Sunday before. Once, long before the encyclical absolving the Jews of any responsibility for killing Christ—long before that—he said it straight out in a sermon. He said to blame the Jews for the death of Christ was absolute nonsense. Remember, this was twenty years ago at least, but years before that encyclical came out. He couldn't have shaken up this diocese more if he'd walked into Aldonari's office and called him a Fascist to his face—which Aldonari was."

"Bishop Aldonari?"

"Well, you know, Mario, I don't mean that literally. But there was no mistaking Aldonari's sympathy when it came to Mussolini. Anybody who could make the trains run on time in Italy and still let the Vatican alone—hell, according to Aldonari, that was practically the Second Coming. So when Sabatine said what he said about the Jews, Aldonari nearly had a stroke.

"And do you know what started all that?" the priest went on, suddenly quite animated. "It was all over Sam Weisberg. Yeah, can you believe it? The thing was, in those days Sabatine had a real passion for golf. The only two things that could keep him off the course were snow and lightning, otherwise he was out there, swinging away. And it must've been on some public course that he met Weisberg. Of course, Sabatine could play any time he wanted to at Westfield Golf Club.

"Apparently, what happened was that he became friendly with Weisberg—how I can't even guess—but he did, and Weisberg probably mentioned something about playing at Westfield. So Sabatine took him—can you imagine?—two or three times from what I heard."

Balzic just shook his head.

"Well, then, apparently Weisberg started making noises about wanting to join Westfield. I don't need to tell you what that club was like right after the war. Every Italian beer distributor, saloon keeper, bartender, and cook in the county was a member. Half of them were members of this parish, and all of them were friends of Muscotti's. Some of them real friends. It's a small miracle that Weisberg wasn't killed the first time he set foot in the parking lot."

"And you mean to tell me that nobody told Sabatine who Weisberg was?" Balzic said.

A FIX LIKE THIS

"Maybe it was because Sabatine was a priest and wasn't supposed to know about such things," Father Marrazo said, shrugging. "Hell, I don't know why nobody told him, but it's obvious that nobody did. Anyway, he got tired of the polite runaround every time he brought the subject up, so he took it right to the membership committee—formally. They listened to him, thanked him for taking an interest in their club, drank some wine with him, all courteous as hell. Then they waited a couple days and sent him a nice, neat little note saying they were sorry but their membership was filled.

"Well, Sabatine didn't just jump to the wrong conclusion. He flew. And apparently, it never occurred to him that there might be some other reason besides Weisberg's ancestry. And I know damn well that it never entered his mind that any one of two or three guys on that membership committee would've considered it an honor to kill Weisberg. And I'm equally certain that Sabatine never suspected for a second that Weisberg was anything but sincere. He'd've probably fainted if he'd heard that Weisberg was laughing himself silly every time he thought of the looks on those guys' faces when Sabatine was in there trying to talk them into letting him join their club.

"Looking back, it's easy to say that Sabatine was naive, or stubborn, or just plain stupid—and that's hard for me to say, especially now. But Sabatine apparently never said a word to anyone. He just had a fit, I mean, he just got righteous as hell, and the very next Sunday he really let those golfers have it, all the ones from the club at what we used to call golfers' mass. I think the last thing he said was something like, 'You insufferable bigots, don't you know or have you ever stopped to think that Jesus was Himself a Jew?' He was about as subtle as a kick in the balls. But even worse was what he did to his hair.

"In those days," Father Marrazo continued, "his hair was fiery red, and very curly, kinky, like Muscotti's used to be, and for some reason he combed it so that it looked like he had sprouted horns. The only possible reason I could give for that was that he had a small reproduction of Michelangelo's *Moses*—he'd had it for years, and he loved it and loved to tell the reason why Michelangelo gave Moses horns—or what he said was the reason—which was that somebody had made a mistake in translating the Hebrew word for light, that the Hebrew for beams of light radiating from Moses' head somehow came out 'horns' in Latin.

"I don't know if that was Sabatine's reason for combing his hair that way or not, but the effect on all those golfers was, well, it just stunned them. They rang Aldonari's phone off the wall, and when Sabatine finished high mass Aldonari was waiting for him; he was right there at the side of the altar.

"He gave Sabatine twenty-four hours to pack and present himself to the cardinal in Philadelphia. I can't remember that cardinal's name, but anyway, he kept Sabatine there for almost six months to make sure he'd emptied his head of what was then flaming heresy. But the day Sabatine came back, he called me, and I'll never forget what he said. He said—without even bothering to identify himself—he said, 'Well, I ate them. I ate my words and I genuflected like a proper little altar boy, but I'll be damned if the Jews are responsible. Who the hell was responsible for all those Jews in Germany—the Lutherans and Communists I suppose?' And then he hung up, just like that. I remember holding my stomach I was laughing so hard. I was thinking, well, hang on to your crucifix, Sabatine's back." Father Marrazo sank back into his chair and shook his head. He seemed to grow smaller. "But now, oh, God...."

"What's the matter now?"

"Well, part of it is that he's got cancer."

"Oh, that's rough," Balzic said. "That's really rough."

"Mario, my friend, that's not the half of it. Not even the half."

Balzic frowned. "I don't know what could be worse—"

"Ho, Lord, Lord, Mario, let me think how to tell you." The priest drank the rest of his wine and motioned for Balzic to do the same, then he stood and turned away from Balzic. When he turned back, his eyes were brimming with tears. He didn't bother to wipe them. He sniffed a couple of times and refilled their glasses, sitting again with a thump.

"Last week, Bishop Conroy called me and ordered me to form an *ad hoc* committee to oversee the auditing of the financial records of St. Jude's parish. He told me to call Kelly from St. Mary's and Marcellino from St. Francis' and to drop everything everybody was doing and meet with the diocesan auditor immediately. All Conroy said was that we were supposed to be there when the auditor went over Sabatine's books and that we were supposed to verify any irregularities. He said he'd gotten some, uh, disquieting information was the phrase he used—yeah, some disquieting information about the mortgage payments from the bank which holds the mortgage on St. Jude's. And that's all he would say.

"So I called Kelly and Marcellino and we met with Jack Raymond, the auditor, and about nine-thirty this morning the four of us went out to St. Jude's unannounced—as Conroy had specified. Well, as soon as I saw Sabatine I wanted to get back in the car. I hadn't seen him in six months or so, and he'd lost so much weight I almost didn't recognize him. And the pain in the man's face, oh, it was awful to look at. It was so obvious the man has only months to live. Maybe not even that long. Weeks perhaps. Shaking hands with him was like grabbing a handful of kitchen matches.

"Well, I stuttered and stammered all over the place, but I

finally managed to say why we were there. He never took his eyes off me the whole time I was trying to tell him, and when I finished he took my hand in both of his and he said, 'Anthony, why did he send you? He had to know how much you'd take this to heart. But don't.' And then he just turned around and let us follow him into his office, and he pointed at the books. They were all laid out as though he'd been expecting us.

"And I asked him if he had been expecting us, and he said, 'No, not you necessarily, but somebody.' Then he said he was very tired and he had to lie down, but if we needed him all we had to do was knock on the wall and he'd come over.

"Now, remember, we still had no idea what we were supposed to be looking for. I suppose I shouldn't be speaking for the others, but I had not the slightest idea. So Jack Raymond went to work, and Kelly and Marcellino were right with him, but I didn't even want to look at the damn stuff. I just kept pacing around, looking at the books on his shelves. He has a fantastic library, the library you'd expect to belong to a man who loves ideas and words. Really great stuff. And I kept looking at his books and remembering what he'd been like in that philosophy class I mentioned earlier and about the hell he'd raised—not for the sake of raising hell. Not at all. He really loved the Church, and he always wanted Her to be better so the people could be better, more loving, more giving, more gracious. And there we were, picking over his books like he was some damn embezzler. It just didn't make sense.

"I mean, what the hell would a man, one of the most honest men I've ever known, certainly the least ambitious for church office—he didn't give a rat's can to be anything more than he was. He never disgraced the Church after he'd been dismissed from the faculty at St. Vincent's. I don't mean that he didn't fight like a tiger for the ideas he discussed with us, but when it was finally decided that he had to go, he went gracefully. The same that time he had to recant to the cardinal in Philly. He went. He ate his words. And he came back still believing that his idea was right—not that he was right but that his idea was—but there was never, never a word out of him about leaving the Church or, or about doing anything to disgrace the Church by disgracing himself. That just wasn't like him. So what the hell were we doing there?

"I mean, would this man who had never disgraced himself when he was young and healthy—what would he be doing now that he's dying of cancer? About his mortgage payments? It didn't make sense. And the longer I stayed there, the less sense it made and the worse I felt...."

Father Marrazo paused to drink some wine. He had been speaking quickly and rather loudly. His face was flushed and there were traces of perspiration on his forehead and upper lip.

"And then I started to think about St. Jude's," Father Marrazo went on suddenly. "Do you know, Mario, what that parish was when he took it over? When he was practically exiled there?"

Balzic shook his head.

"Mass, Mario, he said mass in a garage! A three-bay garage owned by Melago's, that trucking outfit. And the parish was so small that if you put every member of every family in the parish in that garage for one mass, there would still have been room to park a truck in the third bay.

"His altar was a workbench. Think of it, Mario, a workbench! Tools, cans, tires, chains, dirty rags, oil and grease on the floor—the first collection went to buy tarpaulins to cover the floor so the people wouldn't get greasy when they kneeled.

"Hell, he didn't break ground on this building until 1954. He practically begged for the money. And there wasn't one person in the diocese, bishop on down, who didn't know what the man was doing or how hard he was working. He didn't have an assistant until a couple years ago when his health started to go. Now he's got two. But what work he did by himself . . . and there we were, going through his books like he was a thief. I thought I was going to be sick. The idea that he could, or would, do anything for his own gain was absolutely ludicrous.

"And I said so. I told Kelly, Marcellino, and Raymond that we had no right, no reason, no matter what Conroy had said. And I'd no sooner got the words out when Raymond looked up and said, 'We may not have the right, but we have a reason.'

"And do you know what Raymond showed us? He showed us that for the last five months the mortgage payments had increased by twelve hundred and ninety dollars a month. Since November, the payments increased each month by exactly that amount. And we all looked at the figures Raymond showed us and we could see it was true. But I said, 'Well, what the hell's wrong with that? That's great!' But Raymond said, 'There's no explanation for it. There's nothing here to show where the money's coming from.' And I said, 'So the hell with the figures. So it's irregular. So it's unusual. The man's doubled the mortgage payments on his church building, what the hell's wrong with that?' But Raymond kept insisting. 'You don't understand,' he said. 'There's no explanation where he's getting the money.' And I said, 'But why do we have to assume there's something suspicious about it?' And he said, 'Suspicious is your word, Father. All I know is the bank is concerned and the bishop is disturbed.'

"And I just started to howl. It was ridiculous. We go out there looking for who knew what and we find out that Sabatine's doubled his mortgage payments and this damned auditor is talking as though he'd just got the evidence on the greatest swindler in history. And I'm laughing my head off. I'm looking at this pompous-assed auditor and I can't stop laughing, and Kelly and Marcel-lino are starting to laugh too, and then, uh, I feel someone touch my arm.

"It was Sabatine. I hadn't even heard him come into the room. And he looked awful. Just terrible. And everything got quiet, and I finally managed to stop laughing. And he—Sabatine—he looked at me with those eyes so full of pain that it hurt me to look at them, and he said, 'Anthony, the bank has every right to be concerned, and the bishop has every right to be disturbed because it's all a fraud. All that money, that twelve hundred and ninety dollars every month since November, all of it was obtained through a fraud I instigated.'

"Mario, I thought I was going to be sick. . . ." The priest leaned back in his chair and covered his face with his hands and began to sob very quietly. "Damn it!" he cried out, and his shoulders shook.

Balzic jumped up and hurried around the desk and behind the priest. He put his hands on the priest's shoulders. "Let it go, Anthony," he said. "Let it go."

They remained like that for some minutes, Father Marrazo sobbing in his chair and Balzic standing behind him and rubbing and kneading the muscles in the priest's neck and shoulders. Then Father Marrazo began to speak, his words coming in bursts between gasps. "It's so easy to say it's all pride . . . an old man getting old because he starts to think he's indispensable . . . so easy to say he fell for the duty . . . but only 'cause he found out he was dying . . . that's crap, Mario, real crap . . . that man is more than that . . . he just saw his work unfinished . . . he knew it would be done, he knew it . . . but he didn't lose hope . . . and he didn't get smug and arrogant . . . it's not the same, Mario, if you lose your patience, that's one thing . . . if you misplace it, it's not the same as thinking you can't be replaced—or that you won't be . . . my God, Sabatine was too smart for that . . . he hadn't succumbed, he'd surrendered . . . he hadn't given up, he gave himself up—Mario, for Christ's sake, there is a difference . . .

he just lost his perspective . . . it wasn't even that he lost his patience . . . it was his perspective . . . he got out of joint with himself . . . he dislocated his spirit, Mario, that's all. . . ."

Father Marrazo broke down completely. He wept until his eyes were puffed and mucous and spittle dribbled over his fingers. He looked helplessly at Balzic several times, each time trying unsuccessfully to speak. Balzic kept kneading the priest's neck, stopping once to give him his hanky, and then continuing while the priest blew his nose and coughed up phlegm, all the while baffled about the sort of fraud Sabatine had committed which Marrazo was trying so desperately to explain away. Balzic debated with himself whether to ask questions in order that Father Marrazo could get everything out and be done with it or whether to keep silent and let the priest decide if there was more he wanted to say or felt he could say.

Soon, the priest waved his hand and leaned forward, signaling to Balzic that he was feeling better, and Balzic stopped rubbing and went around the desk and back to his chair.

"I'm sorry, Mario."

"For what?"

"For acting like a kid."

"Hey, that wasn't any act and you ain't no kid and don't ever apologize to me for crying over a friend."

"Thank you," the priest whispered.

"Aw come on, Father. I'm going to get embarrassed if you don't cut it out. Here, have a little wine. Make you feel better."

"I think I had too much already. You shouldn't drink when you're depressed. It just makes it worse."

"Yeah, but sometimes it also makes it better. Go ahead."

"Maybe you're right." The priest picked up his glass and sipped what was left in it. Balzic stood and filled both their glasses, still debating with himself whether to prod the priest

A FIX LIKE THIS

to talk more about what Sabatine had done. When he sat down again, he had decided against it. If Father Marrazo wanted to say more, he would, and if he didn't, nothing Balzic could say would persuade him to say anything. The priest could be as close with his thoughts as any man Balzic had ever known. He might let his emotions go now and then, as he had just done, but he was very careful with his thoughts. Now that Balzic thought about it, he was sure this was the first time he had ever heard Father Marrazo reveal anything about another priest or about priests in general. Perhaps he had had too much wine.

"Mario, I think I've said enough for one night. I know I don't have to ask you not to repeat anything I've said. There is one thing though."

"Name it."

"There are bound to be rumors. His housekeeper, Sabatine's, was in and out all the while we were out there. We tried to shoo her away, but she's a, well, never mind what she is. You know her. Mrs. Tuzzi. Gatano's widow. So I'm sure there are going to be rumors. If you hear anything, just do your best—hell, you know what to do."

"Say no more, Father. Anything comes my way, I'll handle it."

"Thank you." The priest paused. "Mario, I really am sorry to put you through this—"

"Forget it, Anthony."

"No, let me finish. You came here obviously with something on your mind. You never just come to pass the time of day. You always have a reason. I'm sorry I couldn't listen to you. But I couldn't. Tomorrow I'll be able to, but tonight I just can't. This has, uh, this has really thrown me. I mean, I just can't imagine Sabatine doing this. And I've really got to sort things out. I have to be able to say something coherent to the bishop. I can't understand why he hasn't called me. . . ."

Balzic stood and drank the last of his wine. He felt suddenly quite drunk. He knew full well that nobody gets suddenly drunk, and the only explanation he could give himself was that he had managed somehow to ignore the gradual sensations of it because he'd been engrossed with what the priest had been saying and going through. He had to hold onto the back of the chair to keep from weaving. "Listen," he said slowly so as not to slur his words, "you don't have to say anything. I understand. And listen, if there's anything else I can do, you know I will."

"I know."

"Well, good night, Father."

"Good night, Mario. And thank you."

Balzic pulled into the driveway of his house and sat in the cruiser for a minute or so after he'd turned off the ignition, trying to comprehend how he'd gotten as drunk as he was. Then he remembered the beer he'd drunk at the bar in Muscotti's, the wine he'd drunk with Dom Muscotti in the back room, and all that wine with Father Marrazo. "Hell," he said aloud, "it's a wonder I'm alive." He stumbled getting out of the car and tripped twice going up the steps to the porch. While he was fumbling for his house key, the door was jerked open by his daughter Marie, and she was smiling wryly.

"Oh, hell, Marie, don't do things like that."

"Hi, Daddy. What things?"

"Never mind. You going to let me in or do I have to stand out here till you tell me what you're going to tell me or whatever?"

"Daddy, are you drunk?"

"Can I come in first?"

"Sure." She backed out of the doorway, and Balzic slid by her, kissing her hair as he passed. Marie closed the door and began taking off his coat. Balzic resisted at first but then let her.

"Are you happy drunk or sleepy drunk?"

"I am definitely not happy drunk. Where's your mother? Where's my mother? Where's your sister?"

"Mom and Grandma are in the kitchen talking. Emily's in bed watching a movie."

"Ho, boy, why don't I ever hear she's in bed reading a book? How come it's always she's in bed watching the tube? I ought to throw that thing—ah, never mind."

Marie stood behind him with his raincoat draped over her arms. "I don't know why she's always watching the tube, Daddy."

"Well what are you so full of? You look ready to bust with something."

"Can't I just meet you at the door and help you take your coat off?"

"Huh, the last time you met me at the door and helped me off with my coat, it cost me forty bucks. Not that I don't appreciate your help. It's your sincerity I can't stand."

"Ohhhh, Daddy."

"Oh Daddy my rump. Come on, what's it going to cost me this time? On second thought, don't tell me. Wait'll I get some coffee, okay?"

"I can wait."

"Okay? Some coffee first, okay?" Balzic slung his arm around her neck and headed wobbily toward the kitchen. "I'll even let you pour it for me. That way, you'll have two things going for you."

She wriggled free of his arm and hurried away, saying, "Wait'll I hang up your coat."

"Okay, so hang it up, hang it up." Balzic loosened his tie and unbuttoned his collar, sputtering out a long sigh.

Marie bounced back into the room, ducked under his arm, and started steering him toward the kitchen.

"Easy now, not so fast, somebody might've moved it. We get going too fast in the wrong direction, it might wind up taking us twice as long to get there."

She giggled. "Daddy, sometimes you're really funny when you're drunk. Especially when you're trying to be serious."

"Ho-ho, backhanded compliments yet. Go 'head, keep working your hustle, daughter. It's a little crude, but it's not bad. Smoothe out the edges, you'll be pretty good in a couple years."

They bumped into the door frame going through the dining room and then came to a halt by bumping into the door frame leading into the kitchen.

"Hello, ladies," Balzic sang out to his mother and his wife. He hoped he didn't look or sound as drunk as he felt.

"Mario, are you all right?" Ruth said.

"Yeah, sure. Just had a little too much to drink, that's all. I'm okay."

"Hey, kiddo," his mother said, "you better sit down before you fall down."

"Hey, I'm not that drunk."

Ruth stood and took him by the arm and pulled him toward the chair she'd just left. "Sit down, Mario. Marie, turn the water on. Come on, Mario, sit down, sit down. My God, look at your eyes. There's no white left at all."

Balzic slumped into the chair Ruth held for him. He rubbed his eyes with his palms and yawned noisily. He shook himself and stretched and then twisted around to look at Marie who was waiting for water to boil so she could make instant coffee for him.

"So whatta you want, Marie? You meet me at the door— you hear that, Ruth? Ma? She meets me at the door, she helps me off with my coat, then she tells me she just wants to meet me at the door and help me off with my coat. D'you believe that? So come on, Marie, let's have the words, I already got the music."

Marie was nearly finished preparing the cup of instant coffee. "It's just nineteen ninety-five, Daddy," she said.

"Ouuu, just nineteen ninety-five, Daddy, that's all. For what? For what am I gettin' grabbed this time?"

"A blazer."

"A which?"

"You know what a blazer is, Mar," Ruth said. "The girls' athletic teams don't get jackets the way the boys' teams do, so the girls decided to buy them for themselves."

"What jackets? What're you talking about?"

"Mar, you know how the school gives jackets with letters on them to the boys who play football and basketball. But the girls don't get anything except a letter. So they got together and decided they'd buy them to shame the school board into doing it from now on."

"Oh, wait a minute. This is goofy. Marie, you mean to tell me you got to have a jacket to remind you of all the time you spent in that swimming pool?"

"Daddy, that's not the point," Marie said, setting the coffee in front of her father.

"What's the point then? I don't need a jacket to remind me I'm a cop. If it was up to me, the only cops in uniform would be traffic duty. Everybody else would be in civvies."

"Daddy, we aren't cops. We're girls who compete for the school and all we get are letters. The boys get letters jackets. We just think we ought to get the same as the boys."

"Ho boy, that's how it starts. Equal strokes for equal folks. He got a pretty uniform, I got to have a pretty uniform . . . next thing you know it's everybody get in step and the next thing after that is you need a bulldozer to make the cemetery—"

"Mario!" Ruth said. "What're you talking about?"

"Nothing, everything. I was just thinking of all the cemeteries scattered all over the world, all of them full of guys who happened to get the privilege of wearing a uniform."

"Aw, Mar, now wait just a minute. This is a school jacket we're talking about, and that's all we're talking about."

"Sure. And all I'm talking about is that's how it all gets started." Balzic stifled a yawn. "School jackets, letters, aw, forget it."

"Mario, it's only right," his mother said. "If the school gives to boys, they should give to girls too."

"Yeah, Ma, I know, I know. But how come I got to be part of it? Marie wants the jacket, the blazer or whatever, why don't she do something? She thinks it's right, then she should do something."

"Like what, Daddy? Like what should we do?"

"What do those band kids do? They want to go march in the Miss America parade or down the Orange Bowl, what do they do—sell pizzas, hoagies, wash cars, stuff like that. Hold a raffle, raffle something off, a TV or something. But I don't like uniforms, and I think to want a uniform is wrong. But I'm not you. You want something to wear to make you special, go ahead, but don't ask me to get it for you—and it doesn't have anything to do with money."

There was silence, the women glancing uncomfortably at each other while Balzic stirred his coffee.

Finally Ruth said, "Maybe that's not a bad idea, Marie, holding a raffle I mean."

Marie frowned and scratched her ankle with her other foot.

"Hey, kiddo," Mrs. Balzic said brightly, "you talk about raffles, guess who won seven hundred dollars."

"Who won seven hundred? I don't know, Ma. Who?"

"Rose Abbatta. Nicolao's widow. You remember."

"Oh, yeah, yeah. I remember her. Good for her. She could use it. She had a lot of rough luck in her lifetime."

"Ho boy, Nicolao was sick so long with that black lung. And then Rosalie, all her life with that poor girl."

"What's wrong with her?" Marie asked. "I don't even know her."

"The people Ma's talking about are old friends of hers," Ruth said. "You've never met them. And the girl she's talking about, Rosalie, she's very retarded."

"Yeah. Is born with brain damage," Mrs. Balzic said. "Have to take care all the time. They got schools for them now, but then it was like a sin to have that happen for you. God was punish you for something. So they never can do nothing without the girl, never go nowhere, all the time have to watch for her. But they been let her go places by herself now. Rose told me Nicky bought her a bike even."

"How old is she?" Marie asked.

"Oh, yoy-yoy, she must be thirty-six, thirty-seven anyhow."

"At least that," Ruth said.

"Is she a mongoloid or something?" Marie asked.

"No," Ruth said. "You can't tell anything from looking at her, except she's sort of, you know, she doesn't have much of a shape. But she had to be watched all the time. A couple times she set fire to the house just playing with matches. And her mother, well, she just never could relax. Except when young Nick got old enough to help her."

"I was just going to say," Balzic said, "he really took care of them after old Nick died."

"Oh sure," Mrs. Balzic said. "He work very hard. Never marry. Always looking out for his mother and sister. He's a good boy."

"Is he still working for the paper, the *Gazette?*"

"He must be," Ruth said. "I don't know why he wouldn't be. He has a really good job there. He's a, oh, what do you call them?"

"Linotype operator," Balzic said, yawning.

"Yeah. That's right. He makes good money."

"Well, yoy-yoy, I tell you something," Mrs. Balzic said, "that's some kind of luck, huh? All those ladies win all that money."

"Huh? What ladies?"

"Well, first was Amelia Motti. You remember, Mario. She's Alfonso's widow. Then was Flora Ruffola, she was marry to Amadie—you know her, Mario?"

"No, Ma, I don't know her."

"Well, okay, then was Sophia Cafasso, she was marry to Domenico—you know her?"

"Uh-uh."

"Sure you do."

"Maybe I do, Ma. I just can't think too clear right now."

"Well, okay. So then was Olivia Tuzzi, Gatano's widow, and now is Rose Abbatta." Mrs. Balzic laughed and slapped the table. "Son of a brick, how you like that? Alla win seven hundred bucks. Yoy-yoy, I like to win sometime, don't you think, kiddo?"

"That'd be nice, Ma."

"Hey, lady, you do all right at bingo," Ruth said.

"Yeah, sure. But seven hundred bucks? How nice!"

Balzic sipped his coffee and scratched the inside of his thigh. "Hey, Ma, d'you say Mrs. Tuzzi won seven hundred too?"

"Yeah. Why?"

"I don't know. I haven't heard her name in a long time, and I could swear I heard it before today someplace. I'll be damned. I can't remember where, but I thought—"

"Mar, I think you better go to sleep," Ruth said. "You look like you're getting ready to fall off the chair."

"Huh? Oh yeah. I better . . . listen, Marie, go tell your girl friends to wash some cars or something. And I'll tell you what. I'll make up the difference, whatever you're short. But if you want that blazer, if you really want it, then I think you ought to try to get it for yourself. Start it anyway. Okay?"

Marie came behind him and hugged him and kissed the top of his head.

Balzic patted her hands and then pulled them apart as he lurched to his feet. He reached out for Ruth's arm and let her direct him into the bedroom. He plopped on the bed and didn't argue when she pulled off his shoes and socks and undid his belt. She struggled to get his pants, coat, and shirt off, giving up finally when Balzic kept falling backward. She left his shirt on.

Balzic was asleep before she left the room, and his last conscious thought was an effort to remember where he'd heard Mrs. Tuzzi's name before today. He couldn't. His mind was flooding with flags and crosses and Stars of David and school monograms and acres and acres of graves....

Balzic awoke with an oppressive fog in his head and the feeling that he had tried to eat tissue paper sometime during the night and hadn't been able to swallow it. He hoisted his feet over the edge of the bed and tried to focus on the alarm clock. He looked at it between rubbing his eyes and yawning, each time disbelieving what he saw. It was twenty minutes after ten.

He could hear pans being washed and rinsed in the kitchen, the sound of soap pads against metal alternating with sudden rushes from the faucet.

He found fresh clothes and went out to the kitchen, hugging his mother as she bent over the sink, and then started up the stairs to the bathroom. He stopped on the third step and asked where Ruth was.

"She's get her hair fix. She just leave."

"How come you let me sleep so long?"

"We try to get you up, kiddo. Ruth try. Me too. But you just no want to get up, that's all."

"Oh." He turned and continued up the stairs, holding onto the wall. He brushed his teeth first to get rid of the tissue-paper taste and then stood in the shower for ten minutes, letting the hot water beat on the back of his neck. By the time he'd finished shaving, the fog in his head was starting to lift.

Downstairs, his mother had coffee and tomato juice waiting for him.

"You want eggs, Mario?"

"No, Ma. I couldn't eat anything. This is enough right here. Just the juice and coffee. Wow, I was really blown away last night. Hope I didn't say anything out of line."

"You?" His mother laughed. "Since when?"

"I don't know. When you get that drunk, you can get out of line anywhere. Even here."

"No, sonny. Not you. Not last night." She was smiling and chuckling as she wiped the pans and put them away.

Balzic drank the juice slowly, savoring it. He was half finished with the coffee when he remembered what he wanted to ask his mother. "Hey, Ma, last night you said something about Mrs. Tuzzi. Remember? When you were talking about somebody winning a raffle or a lottery or something?"

"Yeah, sure I remember. What about?"

"What was it again—four ladies—"

"Five."

"Okay, five. And Mrs. Tuzzi was one of them?"

"Yeah. That's right."

"Well, I was trying to think where I heard her name before."

"What you mean where you heard her name before—you know her all your life."

"Yeah, I know that, Ma. What I mean is, yesterday I heard

her name mentioned before you said it, what you said about her. And I really can't think where."

"Well, what difference it makes, huh, kiddo? She no do nothing bad, that's for sure."

"It doesn't make any difference. I'm just trying to remember."

"Well next time, don't drink so much. Maybe your head work better."

"Ho boy, you're beautiful, you are." Balzic finished his coffee and stood. "Did anybody call me?"

"No. Only one call. I call Rose Abbatta, tell her how good I feel for her."

"How good you feel for her? What for? What happened to her?"

"Boy, kiddo, you really was drunk last night. You forget that too? She win seven hundred dollars, don't you remember?"

"Oh yeah. That. Yeah, sure. Well, she pretty happy, huh? So what's she going to do with it?"

"Oh, she very happy. But I don't ask what she's going to do with. She tells me, but I don't ask. She thinks maybe she buy a new icebox."

"A new icebox? Hell, that's no present. She ought to take a vacation. Ah, that's none of my business where she spends it. It's her money." Balzic started out of the kitchen but came back. "Hey, Ma, I don't know why this is bothering me, but it is. What's Mrs. Tuzzi do?"

"She keep house."

"Doesn't she have a job? I thought she had a job."

"Yeah. That's her job. She keep house."

"For who?"

"For Father Sabatine."

"Out at St. Jude's?"

"Yeah, yeah, that's right. Why?"

"Nothing. I just remembered where I heard her name

before. Yesterday I mean. Father Marrazo mentioned her. Okay. That settles that."

"You happy now, you remember?"

Balzic kissed her on the cheek. "It doesn't make me happy or not happy. I just couldn't remember and it bothered me. You know how that bothers you when you can't remember something you know you know. Listen, I got to go now. I'll see you later, and if I'm going to be late, I'll call you."

"Okay, Mario. Be careful. And be nice. Give somebody a break."

"Give somebody a break? Why today?"

"Oh, I don't know. I just say that, that's all."

"Okay, Ma. I'll give somebody a break today. You and Ruth. I'll stay sober, how's that?"

Balzic learned upon arriving at the station that nothing was going on which couldn't be handled by Desk Sergeant Angelo Clemente. He also learned that Lieutenant Walker Johnson had called to report that a set of fingerprints belonging to someone other than Armand or Tullio Manditti had been found on the door frame of their house and that those prints were being forwarded to the FBI in Washington. That was all the information Johnson had. Balzic screwed up his face thinking about it.

He was just starting out the door when the phone rang. Clemente answered it and waved to Balzic to stop.

"It's Eddie Sitko," Clemente said.

"What's he want?"

"What do I know, he wants to talk to you."

Balzic picked up another phone. "Yeah, Eddie."

"Good morning, Mario."

"Ho boy. When you start in like that, that 'Good morning, Mario,' I can hear trouble coming. What do you want to do this time, Eddie? You want to burn down the hospital to see if your troops can put it out if they ever have to?"

"Be nice, Mario, be nice."

"Hey, Mr. Fire Chief, the last time you asked me to be nice, you told me you were going to hold a foam drill at two o'clock in the afternoon, remember? At the intersection of Main and Market. Remember?"

"I remember very well. That's what I want to talk to you about."

"Oh, Eddie, say not so. You're not going to do that to me again." Balzic closed his eyes and rubbed his temple.

"Mario, we made a mess last time. I mean a real mess—"

"I know, I know. I remember the mess. Traffic backed up six blocks in every direction, foam like meringue a foot deep, and the goddamn phones had smoke coming out of them. You know how long I heard about that?"

"Mario, I heard about it long after you did. But the complaints don't change anything. We got that foam equipment because as long as the goddamn state highway department won't come up with a bypass for Route 66, and as long as gas tankers are using 66, we're sitting on dynamite—"

"Eddie, what do you want me to do—write my state rep? I know what you're saying, and I agree with you one hundred percent. But why do you have to practice on Main and Market? I practice shooting three times a week, but not on Main Street."

"Mario, we've been through all this before—"

"A hundred times."

"But if nobody can move the state people off their asses, then I want my people ready."

Balzic sighed. "So you're really going to do it?"

"Certainly I'm going to do it. Only this time I'm not going to warn anybody except you. I'm not even going to tell my people.

I'm just going to have my wife phone in the alarm, and that way, everybody'll think it's the real thing."

"Oh, Eddie, Eddie, Jesus Christ, don't do this to me."

"It's something that has to be done, Mario. But I want your word you won't tell your people."

"Eddie, for crissake, I'm in the middle of something. I can't fuckin' take time off to go direct the people who're supposed to be directing traffic."

"Mario, it has to be done."

"Look, Eddie, I give you a bad time sometimes, I know I do, but that's because I don't want you to start believing your press clippings. I respect you. I think you're one hell of a fireman. You got more balls than anybody I know. I've seen you do things they wouldn't put in the movies because nobody would believe them, but for crissake, will you do me this favor and hold off for a while? I mean it, Eddie. I'm in the middle of something and I don't even know how big it is yet."

There was momentary silence on the other end. "Is it that bad?"

"I don't really know. I just got a bad feeling. Please hold off for a while. Please? And I promise you, as soon as I get this straightened out, you can hold foam drills to your heart's fucking content—at four-thirty, at eight in the morning, at twelve o'clock Sunday in front of St. Malachy's. You can hold disaster drills until your joint falls off. You can pour ketchup on my head and make me a victim, I won't care. But not now, okay?"

"Okay, Mario, okay. I'll hold off. But not forever."

"Eddie, what can I say? I hope you have to rescue a widow tonight, and she just can't stand it she wants to be so grateful." Balzic hung up and let out a long sigh. "Christ, I should be selling repossessed cars. What a bullshit artist I'm turning into."

"You talking to me?" Clemente said.

"Huh? No, I'm talking to myself. Hey, I'm going to Muscotti's. I got to do another bullshit job on somebody."

"Who?"

"I don't know."

"Then how you—"

"Angelo, when I know what I'm doing, I'll tell you, okay? In the meantime, try to make sure nobody robs the place, okay? We must have close to seven bucks back there in the coffee can."

"Ouuu, sorry I said anything."

"Angelo, what're you, getting old? I can remember when I used to get wise with you, you'd tell me to bug off. All of a sudden you're sorry? So you didn't retire, so what're you doing? Going senile on the job?"

"Okay, so shove it. You got problems, so do I."

"That's better. That's the Clemente we all know and love. See you later, Ang. Anything happens, I'm at Muscotti's."

It was five minutes to noon when Balzic, following a courthouse stenographer and two sheriff's deputies, entered Muscotti's. The bar was crowded with people eating or waiting to eat one of Vinnie's hot sausage sandwiches. The sausage itself was made by Vinnie's Uncle Lou. What Vinnie did was boil and brown the sausage, combine tomato sauce, tomatoes, sweet peppers, onions, thyme, and oregano into a sauce, and then, as he put it, "let the sausage fall in love with the sauce."

Because Vinnie's Uncle Lou kept no schedule about making the sausage, Vinnie had no schedule about preparing the sandwiches. But when he did, word spread quickly. Within a half-hour after he announced that the sausage was ready, that sausage and sauce had made love, it was gone—pounds of it in four-inch portions sliced lengthwise, dripping with sauce, and served on hard rolls.

The amount was never the same because Uncle Lou never delivered the same amount. One morning he might appear with eight pounds. He might not appear again for three days, and then, as likely as not, he would have ten pounds. A day later he might appear with four pounds. Sometimes two weeks would pass before he would appear at all, and he might come empty-handed and roaring drunk, bellowing popular songs from the 1920s in a quaking tenor until Vinnie called a cab for him and gently told him to go home.

Questioned about the erratic delivery of sausage, Vinnie's reply was usually something like, "Hey, my uncle don't only make sausage, he also makes wine. Sometimes he goes down the cellar to make the sausage, he starts tasting the wine, and he forgets what he went down the cellar for. He makes the sausage when he feels like. The rest of the time he sits in the cellar and drinks and thinks about the old country. Hey, I hope when I'm fuckin' seventy-six, I still got enough stomach left to eat it and drink it the way he does, never mind make it. . . ."

Balzic had not come for the sausage. He had come to see if he could meet Dom Muscotti's supposed girl friend, and, if he talked right, to learn if she was—as Mo Valcanas had predicted—merely a sympathetic audience for Muscotti. Balzic didn't know how he was going to go about learning this. He had not even thought of a sensible opening line. But he knew that it was something he had to learn. The presence of Gina Muscotti loomed large in his mind, just as he knew she loomed large in her husband's mind.

Gina Muscotti was a grandmother, frail, fair-skinned, with snowy hair, who looked as though she should be making television commercials for floor wax or vegetable shortening, but she was Italian in her heart and Catholic in her soul. Only God would help her husband if she became convinced that he was treating another woman differently from any other female patron. Balzic shuddered to think that giving a woman booze and twenty dollars a day was hardly Muscotti's custom with female bar patrons.

The bar crackled with the cheer of people drinking and eating food they relished. Adding to that cheer was a truck driver for a beer distributor who had hit a number for fifty cents and was buying drinks all around.

Balzic found a place at the bar near the front door and stood alone for more than five minutes before Vinnie got a break to come and ask if there was something he wanted.

"As long as I'm here, let me have one of those sausages."

"Oh, Mario, honest to God, I just sold the last one to that kid over by the radiator. I didn't have much today. Only six pounds."

"Then give me a beer. Wait a minute, don't run off. Tell me if the Tuscan's girl friend is here."

"The who? Oh." Vinnie rolled his eyes. "Down the other end. You want the beer here?"

"Yeah, sure." Balzic pushed a quarter toward Vinnie and glanced down the length of the bar. He could see only one woman, thirty or so, with straight auburn hair and no makeup. She wore a faded denim jacket over a white tee-shirt. As Vinnie set the beer down and picked up the quarter, Balzic said, "That one standing by herself? At the end?"

"That's her," Vinnie said without moving his lips.

"Oh you're shittin' me. She used to be a caseworker down the Juvenile Home. She worked with Dom's daughter, Louise."

"You got it, pal."

"Christ, she's married. She got three kids."

"Wrong," Vinnie said. "She got two kids, but she ain't married no more. She also don't work down the Juvenile Home either."

"Why, hell, she used to come in here all the time with Dom's kid. Nobody paid any attention to her. Then I didn't see her for a long time. Come to think of it, I haven't seen her down Juvenile for a long time either."

"That's what I'm telling you."

"Oh, I don't believe it. She was Good Samaritan to the world. Used to take those kids home, all that crap. What's she trying to do—save the Tuscan's soul?"

"Mario, I don't know what she's trying to do. I only know what she does. She drinks bourbon and beers all day long and she walks out with at least a twenty. You want to know what she's trying to do, you got to ask her. As for me, I wish she'd get eyes for me or for you or for Iron City Steve, I don't care for who. But she keeps up with Dom, I'm going to get ulcers in my shit." Vinnie started to walk away, but turned abruptly and came back. "You know where she was all that time you didn't see her around?"

Balzic shook his head.

"Mamont. Uh-huh, that's right. The funny farm. She just got out about two months ago. Six months she was in there. I don't know what you can do with that, but I'm telling you 'cause sometimes she don't make too much sense—that's if you're really going to talk to her."

"I don't know where I'm going yet, Vinnie. But thanks for telling me." Balzic sipped his beer and mulled that one over. Mamont State Hospital. Six months on the farm and out to twenty a day and free boilermakers, compliments of the number-two numbers banker in the county who years ago announced his impotence. A hundred and twenty a week or more and all the booze she could handle—for what? For sympathy? Huh, Balzic said to himself, maybe she's a faith healer. Nah, no way.

If she could cure that problem with faith, she'd be filling more stadiums than Billy Graham.

Balzic had not realized it but he'd been staring at her, and when his eyes refocused, he saw that she was returning his stare. There was no hostility in it, nor even discomfort. What he saw was bemused curiosity. He turned his face away and pretended that he'd found an itch on his neck. Then he turned his back and took a long drink of beer. He tried to think how to approach her and then found himself trapped in a debate whether he really had any business approaching her at all. This was personal, he said to himself, but then he said, it could become the worst that Muscotti feared. And if Muscotti feared it, there was good reason for lots of other people to start fearing it. Still, it was personal. And it was one thing to be summoned by neighbors to end a family argument before it turned into assault or worse, but it was something else again to invite yourself into the middle of a potential family argument—no matter that this potential family argument could wind up in the U.S. Attorney's office. Oh, hell, he groused to himself, nobody even knows what Gina Muscotti's thinking about. All she did was call Vinnie to find out how business was at the bar. Who am I kidding? Balzic thought. She calls Vinnie, that's got to be a first. She knows something's up. She knows....

Balzic felt someone brush against his shoulder and then felt someone drawing a stool near to him.

"Hi, Chief," the voice said pleasantly.

Balzic turned around while in the midst of swallowing beer. He nearly choked. It was her. He gagged and coughed and felt his eyes bulging.

"Easy," she said, patting him on the back while he bent over the bar and coughed violently. "Don't hurt yourself," she said, laughing. "If I'd've known I'd cause all this, I wouldn't have come."

"It's all right," Balzic said after his coughing passed. "It just went down the wrong way. You didn't cause it."

"Chief, don't lie. I saw you staring at me."

"You did? Yeah. Well, I guess I was."

"Honestly, you too? Everybody's staring at me lately. I'm going to get crazy again if this keeps up."

"Crazy again?"

"Oh, Chief, come off it. I saw Vinnie telling you."

"You saw Vinnie telling me what?"

"That I just got out of the zoo a couple months ago."

"You could hear that from clear down where you were?"

"I didn't say I could hear it. I said I could see it."

"You could see it?"

She nodded.

"You must be some kind of lip reader."

"I don't mean that. I mean I could see the exchange between you two. I got the vibrations. I saw the auras."

"The what?"

"The auras. Don't you know that people give off electrical charges?"

"I know we got a lot of electricity in us. I don't really understand—"

"Well, it doesn't matter. But one of the definitions of aura is that it's a current of air caused by a discharge of electricity, and when people give off their electricity, they disturb the air around them and create color. Haven't you ever seen a painting of a saint?"

"Well, sure I have—"

"Well why do you think painters put them there? You think it was something the Church invented? To make people think saints were special? I mean, sure they're special now, but see, a long time ago, before painters began to work exclusively for the

Church, they used to paint everybody like that, not just saints and martyrs, because, well, a long time ago people believed everybody had one."

"You might be right," Balzic said. "I don't know enough to argue."

"Oh, you can't argue at all. This is true. It's how I got my head together. I used to see auras all the time around people's heads, but then I found out that this was true historically, that people used to believe it, and if I hadn't found that out I'd still be in the zoo wiping old ladies' asses and mopping up their vomit."

"This got you out, got your head together?"

"Sure. Because once I found out it was true a long time ago, then I knew it was still true and I wasn't seeing things. I mean I was seeing things, but—"

"Well, you just lost me there. 'Cause a long time ago people used to believe the world was flat, but just 'cause they believed it didn't make it true. I mean, we know it ain't flat."

"Sure, but the world's not flat. I mean, we know the world's not flat because of science. And science is the very thing that drove away the idea that people had auras. I mean, it wasn't scientific. Nobody could measure it, and if you can't measure something, then it's not scientific to talk about."

Balzic shrugged. "I guess so. In some respects."

"Of course," she said, laughing, and then she put her hand, her palm with her fingers together, on the middle of Balzic's back. She kept it there for two or three seconds, her eyes sparkling, her lips parted, her head canted. "Don't be afraid," she said after taking her hand away.

"I'm afraid?"

"Sure. You think I'm going to tell you something destructive. And I am—in a way. I mean, you can't ever tell anybody anything constructive without telling them something destructive. They go together like black and white. But everybody always gets scared at first until they know that."

"Okay, I'll play," Balzic said. "What do I think you're going to destroy that's going to shake me up so much?"

"What else? Your ideas."

"Like which ideas?"

"Well, like the one that I can know you were afraid while you were looking at me with this great stone face that says, 'Hey, I'm tough. I'm imperturbable.'"

"And you knew I was, uh, afraid because of my aura, is that it?"

"Well, I felt your fear in your spine."

"Oh."

"Just oh? Is that all? You don't have to be so damned reserved or polite. You can laugh or argue or do anything you want. Except don't be a goddamn American on me."

Balzic laughed. "That's pretty hard."

"Oh, you don't know how hard. For crissake, a third of the world is American. Everybody who believes that time is a line that goes from left to right and can be numbered from one to ten is American. And you believe that. It's practically in your genes. And you know who are the worst about that? Those goddamn psychiatrists. They're so goddamn wrapped up in their little left-to-right, one-to-ten world, they're convinced that anybody who doesn't believe in that is crazy. And they almost had me believing it! And when I tried to tell them about time being an orbit and a revolution, a circle with no beginning and no end, they put me in the rubber room and shot me full of dope."

"They shot you full of dope? The psychiatrists?"

"Sure. There's no difference between heroin and Thorazine. Only chemically. It's all dope. Anything that makes you not want to find out who you are is dope."

"Uh, what's booze then? I mean, what's in those glasses in front of you?"

"Oh, see what a bastard you are! You look for contradictions," she said, laughing impishly and touching Balzic's back again with her palm. "Just because I use dope in a glass doesn't mean I don't know I'm using it or don't understand why I'm using it."

"Why are you using it?"

"Oh, look how serious you say it! Everything coming off you looks like something Rembrandt painted, all dark brown. If he were here now, he'd probably want you to go home and pose for him."

"Yeah, well, so how come you use it? Come on, don't give me any more stuff about my auras or whatever the hell they are. How come you take dope in a glass?"

She took her hand away slowly and touched Balzic's cheek with the back of her index finger. "You promise not to arrest me?"

"Aw be serious, willya?" Balzic snorted a laugh.

"I won't be serious, but I will be sincere. You have to promise."

"That I won't arrest you?"

"Yes. Absolutely."

"Okay, I promise." Balzic smiled and then caught Vinnie's eye and motioned for him to refill their glasses.

She said nothing while Vinnie was doing this, and Vinnie said nothing to either of them. He refilled their glasses, took Balzic's money, brought the change, and left quickly without a word.

"See how well Vinnie understands auras?" she said.

"Who? Vinnie?"

"Sure. See how he knew not to intrude?"

"Well, I don't know if it's because he understands auras. But I know he understands people pretty good."

"Oh, he won't admit it, but he understands," she said.

"So, uh, now that I promised not to bust you—what's your name by the way?"

"Oh, my name, my name. We were having such a good talk and now you want to spoil it with a fact." She grimaced. "Now I don't know whether I ought to tell you why I drink dope. Even though you promised." She pressed the heel of her hand against her forehead and hit herself gently twice, thinking for a long moment. "Okay. My name is Mila Sanders Rizzo. Feel better now? Is that enough, or do I have to go through the whole bit—name, age, marital status, social security number, phone number, address? Why does every conversation have to start out like an interrogation, like everything has to start according to the Geneva Convention . . . oh, wow, I hate that. Every time I talk to Dom, the first thing I have to say is where my children are, who's watching them, do I trust them, what time do I have to pick them up."

"Well what do I call you?"

"I don't care. Call me yoo-hoo, only when you say it, think of it as being spelled y-o-u-w-h-o. Think of it as a nickname for my full name, which is you-who-are."

"Does that have capital letters?"

"Oh, God," she said, groaning, "don't you Americans ever give up? Put capital letters on it if it makes you feel better, I don't care."

They were both laughing by the time she finished talking. She paused to sip her bourbon and followed that with a sip of beer.

"So come on," Balzic said, "I want to hear why you take your dope in a glass."

"Okay, but remember your promise."

"I remember."

"Well, I have certain hangups. One of them, the biggest I guess, is that my father owned a bar."

"So? Lots of people who own bars have children."

"Yes, but you see, I'm—I'm still trying to get my head together. And I keep trying to find out where I came from, what I was before I was. I'm trying to go back in order to get here, I think it's crucial to know what I was before so I can know what I am now."

Balzic rubbed his chin. "And you're finding that out in here? Taking dope in a glass?"

"This is the best place! I come in here, it's like a womb. And then it's like infancy. All these glasses need are rubber nipples on them. And then during the day when I talk to Dom I'm in puberty and adolescence. And then later on, when everybody goes home at night, when there's only Dom and me in here, then I'm almost me—where I am now. And then when I give him some head, it's everything all at once, it's—"

"When you give him what?"

"You heard me. Oh, come on, don't look so innocent. Don't tell me you don't know what I'm talking about."

"Oh, I know what you're talking about," Balzic said, feeling himself blush. "I just never heard anyone say it so matter of fact before, that's all. No, that's not it. You just surprised me."

"Well it's no big deal. I mean, everybody knows it, so what's to hide?"

"Uh, listen, uh, maybe you shouldn't be telling me these things. I mean, they're, uh, pretty personal, you know?"

"Well, Christ, everything's personal! There isn't anything you can say that isn't personal. Talking about the weather is personal. Somebody says, 'You think it's going to rain?'—what do you think they're saying? They're making noises that say, 'Hey, I'm harmless. Let's talk.' And if that's not personal, what is? Besides, you're lying when you say you don't want to hear this. 'Cause this is exactly what you do want to hear. You think I don't know that? I mean, why'd you come in here and talk to Vinnie about me if you didn't want to know what was going on?" She spoke quickly but softly and there was not even annoyance in her face or tone.

"Well, uh, I guess you got me," Balzic said.

"Of course I do. But I'm not trying to get you. I just want you to be as sincere and honest with me as I'm being with you. Is that so much to ask?"

"No."

"Well, then why don't you give yourself a break? I mean, if you want to know how to handle this, then you better know what there is to know, don't you think?"

"How do you know I want to handle it?"

"Oh, stop it, will you please? You're the chief of police. Dom's, well, you know what he is better than I do. Everybody knows his wife. And everybody, including you and Dom, is scared shitless that she's going to find out and want to get some kind of silly revenge or something just because I'm using him to grow up on. Everybody thinks he's using me to prove what a man he still is. But that's a load. I'm using him a hundred times more than he'll ever think of using me. Whose idea do you think it is that he gives me all the money? You think it's mine? He's showing off. And I let him because that's the only way he can make any sense of me. But I don't want his money. I haven't spent a penny of it. It's all in the bank. All he has to do is give me the slightest indication that he regrets giving it to me, and I'll tell him how soon he can have it back. There's no big deal."

"Uh, how about running that down again?" Balzic said. "I'm a little confused."

"Well how many ways do I have to say it? I'm into where my head is. Right now. I have to find out what I'm doing, and

I'm using Dom to help me. Because my father owned a bar. Because—"

"What happened to your father?"

"Nothing happened to him. He's still alive and healthy as hell. He just can't help me, that's all. He's always making judgments about what I'm supposed to be. He won't ever just let me be who I am—if I could ever find out. But if I'm ever going to get myself together, then I have to have a substitute. It's called acting out. All those creepy psychiatrists know about it. They're the ones who told me about it. So just because I understand it—no. Just because I really do it, really do act it out, everybody gets excited. And it's really no big deal."

"Not even if Dom's wife decides it is? I mean, suppose she thinks it's the biggest deal there is. Like adultery."

"Oh, come on. Who knows better than her that he isn't capable of adultery? I just told you, giving him head is like sucking shots and beers with nipples on the glass. He never has an erection. He can't! Christ, afterward, he cries every time."

Balzic shook his head and sighed. "Wait a minute. Don't you understand that that might not make any difference to her?"

"Well that's her hangup, not mine. God, I've got enough of my own. I can't handle mine and hers too."

"Well okay then. Just who the hell is supposed to handle it? Me?"

"Isn't that what this whole conversation is about? Isn't that what you want to do? Handle this? Protect everybody? 'Cause if it isn't, then you're sure sending off some funny auras."

"Oh, Christ, we're back to them again," Balzic said. "Vinnie! Hey, Vinnie! Give us a couple more here."

Vinnie approached, grinning slyly. "So how we doin', Mario? Everything okay? How 'bout you, kid? You okay?"

"I'm okay," Mila said. "But I don't know about the chief here. He's confused. There's gray around his head a foot high."

Balzic started to say something but was stopped when he felt someone touch him on the left shoulder. He turned and was confronted by Brownie Cercone, somber and scowling.

"We got problems," Cercone said. "Come here."

Balzic followed him to the far end of the bar.

"Listen, Balzic, I didn't want any part of this, I want you to know that."

"Any part of what? What're you talking about?"

"What do you think I'm talking about? What did you talk about yesterday?"

"With Dom?"

"Sure with Dom. D'you think the fuckin' Pope?"

"So okay. What's the problem?"

"Dom did what you said. He stuck me on Tullio out the dump."

"And?"

"He split. I lost him."

"How the fuck could you lose him at the dump?"

"Not so loud for crissake. Just listen and I'll tell you." Brownie's eyes darted over Balzic's shoulders. "He told me he had to go take a crap. So I'm with him all day, right behind him from the time he wakes up this morning, but I ain't going in the can with him. I mean, Jesus Christ, I got stink all over me from that dump—"

"Forget that. What happened?"

"He goes in the can. I'm waiting and I'm waiting. Ten minutes goes by, and I holler in at him. I say, 'Hey, d'you have a fuckin' heart attack or you jackin' off or what're you doing?' Nothing. So I open up and he's gone. Turns out there's another door in the back so guys can get in from outside without going through the office. So I start running around looking for him, but one of the pickers tells me the fat-ass climbed on the back of a packer when it was pulling out."

A FIX LIKE THIS

"Whose truck?"

"Nobody knows," Cercone said. "What do you think I'm telling you we got problems for? Jesus, don't you think that's the first thing I'm going to ask? There was only one guy saw him going, and that guy's just off a boat last year. He can't read English. He don't know what that fuckin' print means on the truck. He also don't know one truck from another."

"Oh for crissake. Does Dom know yet?"

"No. I ain't been able to find him either."

"Well you're having some kind of day, Brownie, I'll tell you that."

"You can't tell me nothing. You think I don't know Dom's gonna shit hand grenades when I tell him?" Brownie winced and whistled softly. "You know, I thought this was a bunch of nothing yesterday. Real nothing. But being around that fat-ass all day, now maybe I think he's really gonna do something. But listen, Balzic, you got to know this is something those two whales did on their own. The rest of us didn't have anything to do with it."

"I know that."

"Well then what the fuck was all that noise you gave Dom yesterday? What the fuck was that about?"

Balzic turned away without giving Cercone a reply. He paused at the door, turned back to Mila Sanders Rizzo, and said, "I got to go. But I want to talk to you some more."

"I'm right here every day," she said, smiling. Then she put both her hands together over her head and made sweeping motions as though she were doing a breaststroke. Then she pointed at Balzic and laughed.

"Oh fuck," Balzic said under his breath and hurried out to his cruiser.

Balzic scrambled out of his cruiser at the station and trotted into the duty room, loosening his tie as he went. Sergeant Angelo Clemente looked up, startled, and swiveled around on his chair.

"What's up?"

"Get on the phone. Call every fourth guy and tell him to call the other three. Everybody doubles up until further notice; extra shift in plain clothes."

"What do I tell them?"

"Just tell them to get the fuck in here. And I don't mean two hours from now."

"Mario, I hope you know what you're doing. That's a lot of overtime. Council ain't going to go—"

"Do it, Angelo! You let me worry about City Council."

Clemente shrugged and shook his head several times, his eyes half closed, his lips pursed. He muttered something else, but he rolled his chair over to one of the phones and started dialing.

Meanwhile, Balzic went to the radio console and opened the switch to all channels.

"All units, all personnel," he began. "Priority, priority. Apprehend and arrest one Tullio Manditti, male, Caucasian, age approximately thirty-five, height approximately five feet seven inches, weight approximately two hundred and eighty, ninety pounds, build extremely obese, usually wears and was last seen wearing coveralls. Street charge is material witness. Bring him to the station. Repeat, bring him to the station. Do not, repeat, do not remand him to a magistrate. Manditti may be armed. Do not let his build fool you. He is agile and extremely strong. Do not attempt to apprehend him by yourself. Call for backup. Repeat, call for backup . . . and for the rookies and all you other dumb fuckers out there, that means I want Tullio Manditti in here but you ain't supposed to try to make the collar by yourself. One on one, he'll get you off your feet and sit on you. Then you're his. If you do get stuck, mace him, but whatever you do, don't get close enough to use a baton. Guaranteed, you'll lose. . . ."

Balzic repeated the call and asked for and got confirmation of reception from all beat patrolmen and mobile units. Then he stood and went over beside Clemente. "How we doing?"

"I got two more to go. No problems so far. Lot of bitching, but no problems."

"Good. Stay with it. I want them all here."

Balzic went to another phone and dialed Muscotti's. Vinnie answered.

"This is Balzic. Are Soup, Digs, and Brownie there?"

"Just Brownie."

"How about Dom?"

"He won't get here for another fifteen or twenty minutes. Why?"

"If Tullio Manditti should happen to roll in there—which I doubt—you tell him to stay there and then you call me, got it?"

"Yeah, sure, Mario."

"Okay, let me talk to Brownie."

There was a whooshing sound, as though Balzic had had a clam shell shoved against his ear, and then a thump. Then Vinnie's voice called out to Brownie Cercone. More whooshing and scraping followed.

"Yeah?" Brownie said.

"Balzic. You get Soup and Digs and get on the street. Talk to all your people. I want Tullio, you understand?"

"Hey, now wait a minute, Balzic. I ain't no fuckin' beagle."

"Wait my ass. You turn beagle. You get oh the street and start looking and talking. And when you find him, you stay with him until you call me, you hear?"

"Oh for crissake—"

Balzic hung up without letting him finish. Then he waited.

An hour later his entire force, except for the men already on duty, was assembled in the duty room. Few of them looked Balzic in the eye. There was much grumbling and subdued cursing until Balzic reminded them of the overtime pay. Then they grew quiet and attentive and some of them even looked eager. Balzic worried about the eager ones but tried to put them out of mind while he told them who he wanted and why.

Two hours later, after calling Walker Johnson of the state police and District Attorney Milt Weigh and asking for whatever assistance they could give, Balzic was still pacing around the duty room. He'd allowed Angelo Clemente to go home because Clemente's feet made it impossible for him to walk more than three or four blocks without having to rest for ten minutes and because his wife was using the family car to take her mother shopping.

Sergeant Vic Stramsky had taken over the desk, and he was being quietly proficient, handling all the nuisance calls without bothering Balzic.

By five o'clock it appeared to Balzic, who had quit pacing and was now sitting at one of the front desks with his feet up, that Tullio Manditti may as well have been in Florida. Balzic scowled up at the clock above the radio console and drummed his fingers on his stomach.

"Hey, Vic, see if my arithmetic's right."

"Huh?"

"Just add something. Right there, on the blotter." Balzic paused and pinched the bridge of his nose. "Me and you and Angelo. That leaves thirty-three of our people. Okay, so then we got Soup, Digs, and Brownie. How many people you figure they got?"

"All over Rocksburg and Southwest Rocksburg, and

Westfield Township? Hell, they got to have ten or twelve apiece. More than that."

"I figure it's more like twenty apiece."

Stramsky shrugged. "Maybe so."

"Okay, so if only half of them are out looking and listening, that's thirty, thirty-five more, right?"

"Yeah, that would be about right."

"Okay, so then we got two mobile units from the state, one from Westfield in Westfield, and then we got three undercover nares plus Carraza and Dillman from Weigh's office."

"Let me add it up here." Stramsky scratched the hair above his ear and started figuring on the blotter. After a moment he said, "I get between seventy and seventy-five, depending on how many of Dom's street people are cooperating."

"Yeah. That's what I came up with," Balzic said. He leaned back in his chair and kneaded his hands. "Just think, Vic. I mean, imagine it. Seventy, seventy-five people looking for one guy, a fuckin' dirigible on feet, in a town this size for—what is it now—three hours?"

"At least that long."

"And nobody sees him. Now what do you figure the odds got to be on that? Hell, I didn't even include the security people at the hospital." Balzic shook his head. "That's three, four more, right?"

"No. There's just two guys up there now. The other two won't come on until the nurses start changing shifts. That's at eleven."

"Even so, Christ, the sun is shining, everybody knows what he looks like. I mean, who could miss a walking mountain, even if it is short?"

Stramsky shrugged and was about to say something when the phone stuttered on the switchboard. He plugged in the line and listened for a short time. Then he said, "Mario, I think somebody seen him."

"Huh?" Balzic lurched forward on his chair and grabbed the phone. "This is Balzic. Go ahead."

"This is Mrs. Kwalick in Emergency."

"Yes, ma'am, how are you?"

"I'm fine, thanks. But I think you better come up here. We just had an admission, a man in his early forties named Francis Dulia, and he's in very bad shape. He has at least a dozen fractures, probably more, but no lacerations or abrasions. The man who brought him in says that he was beaten up."

"I'm on my way," Balzic said, dropping the receiver on the hook and scurrying toward the door. "That fat bastard did it. That sonofabitching lard-ass got him. All these people looking, and he got to him anyway. . . ."

"I did not make a thorough examination," the doctor said. He was Indian, tall, slim, with long, slender hands. His accent was British. He gestured apologetically. "I made really just a cursory examination and then I alerted radiology and the resident surgeons. I then requested that a neurosurgeon be summoned."

"Uh-huh. Well what did it look like to you?"

"There had been severe concussion, and quite possibly fractures of both the left parietal and temporal bones—"

"The skull?"

"Yes. Here." The doctor pointed to two places on his own head, just above the left ear and then slightly above and behind the ear. "His eyes responded very poorly, and there was extensive bleeding from the left ear. From the swelling and from the position of his teeth and chin, it was clear his mandible was fractured—his jaw. Excuse me, I will speak in layman's terms. His left collarbone was obviously fractured. That was visible. I did not even have to touch it."

"What else?"

"The upper left arm was fractured in at least two places, as was the forearm and quite possibly the wrist. Again, that was clear to the eye from the position of the left arm. His left knee was extremely swollen, indicating fractures there. There were other swellings up and down the length of his left leg, from the hip to the foot. But there was something very curious."

"What's that?"

"There were not even abrasions of the skin. I admit that I am relatively inexperienced, but I have never seen anything like these injuries. I do not see how it is possible to have that many fractures without laceration—in fact, very little evidence of trauma except for the contusions. I don't understand it."

"Well, unfortunately I do," Balzic said.

"Then perhaps you can explain it to me."

"Listen, do you know the county coroner?"

"Dr. Grimes?"

"Yeah. You get him to explain it to you. He knows all about it. He's the one who explained it to me. Okay, Doc, thanks. Oh, what about the guy's wife?"

"Understandably, she was quite hysterical. I prescribed Nembutal for her."

"Can I talk to her?"

"Not for three or four hours at least. She was much too active physically and vocally. My first prescription only slowed her somewhat."

"What about the guy who brought him in? Where's he?"

"Oh, I don't know that. You should ask Mrs. Kwalick."

Balzic nodded and patted the doctor on the arm. He headed out of the office to find Mrs. Kwalick, stopping at each of the treatment rooms and leaning in to ask if she was there.

At the last treatment room, he was hailed before he leaned in by a grizzled, powerfully built, elderly man wearing a tee-shirt and green trousers. His soiled green cap was dotted with outdated United Mine Workers union buttons. He had no teeth, and he was rolling a cud of tobacco from cheek to cheek.

"Ain't you the chief of police?"

"Yes. What can I do for you?"

"I brung him in. Him and his missus. The fella that had the hell beat out of him."

"Ah, you're the man I'm looking for," Balzic said, putting his hand on the man's shoulder and steering him gently toward the office where moments ago he'd spoken with the Indian doctor.

"Have a seat, Mr., uh—"

"Harsha. Andrew T. That's for Theodore. Just call me Andy."

"Well, Andy, are you a neighbor?"

"I live next door to them if that's what you mean, but I ain't their neighbor."

"How close is next door?"

"It's twenty-one feet from my house to my property line. It's forty feet from the property line to their house. They say it's fifty feet. *He* says. She never said nothing about it. That's why I ain't their neighbor. I got a lawyer working on it right now. I don't know what the hell he wants with that other ten feet, but he ain't gonna get it, and right now, it looks like he ain't gonna be able to use it even if he does get it, which he ain't, and—"

"Uh, Andy," Balzic interrupted him, "I'm sure your lawyer'll take care of your property rights, uh, so just tell me what happened—if you know."

"Huh? Oh, I know what happened all right. I seen the whole thing."

"Okay. Exactly what did you see?"

"Well, I come home from work, and I was standing in my kitchen just ready to pour myself a shot and a beer, to cut the dust, you know, and then I was going to go out and clean up the mess them goddamn raccoons made. They—"

"Go on," Balzic prodded him.

"Well, Dulia come out the back door of his house, and I thought he was gonna come over and start breaking my hump about the goddamn property line again. So I was getting ready for him. I had a few things I was gonna let him have, but as soon as I could see his face close up, I could see he looked real confused and kinda scared, sorta all flustered like he didn't know where he was. I seen guys coming up out of the shafts like that after old Mother Earth shakes her ass a little bit. You know, they made it out okay, but they're still pretty shook up.

"So, anyway, he starts to look around like he's trying to find something. Then he looks up at the woods behind us. Then he sneaks over to the far corner of his house and peeks around the corner. He pulls back real quick. Then he runs, sorta tippy-toe, over to the other corner, the one closest to me, and he peeks around that.

"So now I'm thinking this is pretty comical, so I'm really watching him. I got a shot in my hand and I didn't even drink it until it was all over. Anyway, all of a sudden he starts to run up toward the woods, and he gets only, oh, maybe four or five steps when this thing come flying from down around the front of his house, I guess, and smacks him right square in the back and down he goes. And, oh, you can see he's hurting. His face is all twisted up, and he's having a hard time catching his breath."

"What was this thing that hit him?"

"Well, I couldn't tell right then. Not until the fat guy picks it up."

"Then what?"

"Well, then I could see it was a bat, you know, a baseball bat, except it had something white wrapped all around the end. Looked like a towel but I couldn't be sure."

"Go on."

"Well, next thing I know this real fat guy, I mean really fat, he comes up and grabs the bat and he whacks Dulia across the leg with it. He don't say nothing. He just whacks him. Then he leans down close to Dulia and says something to him, but I can't hear it. But I heard Dulia say, 'Oh, Christ, don't hit me again,' something like that. But that guy whacked him anyway. Right here." Harsha pointed to his left forearm.

"You heard them through the window?"

"No. I had the window open a couple inches. I just painted my kitchen the last couple days. Just did the last coat on the woodwork yesterday. That's how come I had the window open."

"Okay. Go on."

"Well, the fat guy whacks him again. Right across the side of the knee. Right here." Harsha stood and pointed to the outside of his left knee. "He was laying on his side like this." Harsha got on the floor on his right side and propped himself on his right forearm and held up his left arm as though to cover his face. Then he scrambled up and demonstrated as though chopping wood with an imaginary ax. "The fat guy was whacking him like this, see?"

"I see," Balzic said.

"Then he leans down and says something else to Dulia. But I can't hear that either. All I can hear is Dulia begging him not to hit him again. But the fat guy don't pay no attention. He straightens up and whacks him again. Right here." Harsha pointed to the outside of his left wrist. "And Dulia is screaming like hell and then he starts to bawl."

"And you were just watching all this?"

"Sure I was watching it. What do you think I'm telling you?

Oh. You mean how could I just stand there and watch it? Oh, hell, I seen fellas pinned under tons of shale, man. Just their head sticking out. I seen guys with half their face blowed away, their guts hanging out, their legs and arms maybe four, five feet away from them—over in Italy during the war. It don't bother me."

"I understand. Well, go on. What happened then?"

"Well, this fat guy leans over again and says something else. I can't hear him. But this time, Dulia, he starts hollering something which I couldn't make no sense out of. He starts hollering, he says over and over, 'It couldn't lose. It wasn't supposed to lose.'"

"'It couldn't lose? It wasn't supposed to lose?' He said exactly that?"

"Yup. I heard it clear as a bell. He must've said it, oh, four, five times," Harsha said. "And this fat guy, he whacks him two more times. Right here on the hip. Oh, he's really bringing it to him. And Dulia's screaming. Then it's the same thing all over again. 'Bout five more times. He'd lean down and say something to him, then he'd up and whack him, all up and down his left side."

"How long did all this take?"

"Huh? Oh, not more than a couple minutes. Everything I told you so far. Maybe not even that long. No time at all."

"Okay. Go on."

"Well, by this time Dulia's all cried out. I mean, his face still looks like he's crying, see, but there ain't no noise. So then this fat guy, he puts the bat down, you know, leans it against his leg, and he takes out a hanky and wipes his face and neck. He's really got a sweat going. Then he leans down real quick, and Dulia says something I can't hear. He talks for a real long time, oh, maybe five minutes, and the fat guy's leaning over and listening real intent and wiping his face. Then, all of a sudden, he shoves the hanky back in his pocket and he hollers, 'You motherfucker, I'm gonna beat your fuckin' brains out. I wasn't, but I'm going to now.'"

"He said exactly that?" Balzic said.

"Just what I said. It was only the second time he said anything I could hear. And he kept saying it. And he starts in whacking him again, and he steps over him and whacks him four or five times real fast. Once here"—Harsha indicated where by drawing his thumb downward over his left collarbone—"and at least three times on the head. I couldn't tell where exactly, 'cause by this time the fat guy is between me and Dulia, but I knew where when I went over to Dulia after."

"Then what happened?"

"Well, then the fat guy, he just turned around cool as you please and walked off toward the front of the house. Then I heard a car start up and drive off. That's when I went over to see how Dulia was. Soon as I got close, I could see the blood coming out of his ear, and I knew I had to get him in here real fast. I couldn't wait for no ambulance. So I backed my truck up the lawn and I went and got some blankets and I laid him in the back as easy as I could and I brung him in. Then I went and got his missus from where she works."

"And that's it?"

"That's it. That's everything. I didn't leave nothing out."

"Okay. Now, is there any doubt that you'd recognize this fat guy again if you saw him, I mean positively recognize him?"

"Shoot, you couldn't mistake him. Not that lard-ass."

"Did he ever see you?"

"He never even looked in my direction. Not once."

"How far away were you?"

"I told you before. My house is twenty-one feet from the—"

"Yes, I know. But where were they? How far from Dulia's house?"

"Oh, they was maybe ten yards from the back corner of his place and, lemme see, maybe five yards over toward my place."

"And you had a clear, unobstructed view?"

"Sure. There's nothing but the fence I put up 'bout two months ago."

"What kind of fence? How high?"

"Regular chain-link fence. You can see through it. I bought it out at Sears and put it in myself. Three feet above ground and a foot below ground. I was looking over it at the fat guy, but I had to look through it to see Dulia."

"But there was nothing else between you and them, no trees or hedges or anything like that?"

"Not a damn thing 'cept the fence."

"Okay, Andy, that's enough about that. Now what can you tell me about Dulia?"

"Aw, he was okay until he hurt his back. Then he couldn't work no more, and he started to get moody as all hell."

"When did he hurt his back?"

"Oh, must be over a year now. He was in the hospital a long time. Five or six weeks. Oh, he was a mess. They took a piece of bone out of his hip and put it in his back, and then he got an infection or something. He looked like hell when he finally come home. And then it wasn't too long before he had to go back in. But I never had no trouble with him before that. They been living there for ten years, and he never said a goddamn word about the property line till after he come out of the hospital the second time. Then that's all he talked about. One time I said to him, 'What the hell you think's under there, oil or something?'"

"How about the people on the other side of him? Did he have any trouble with them?"

"I don't know nothing about that. There's just an old lady living there, and she ought to be in the county home. But I don't think Dulia could've given her a bad time 'cause his missus used to look out for her, that old lady I mean. I seen her taking food over lots of times and I think she used to wash her clothes."

"Uh-huh. Well, what else do you know about him? How were they living if he wasn't working? Was he on workmen's compensation?"

"Yeah. Then his wife works at that supermarket. She's a checkout. They was getting by, I guess. Not like when he was working, naturally. He was a bricklayer. You know how much those guys make an hour. So it was a comedown, but hell, they didn't have no kids."

"Did you ever hear him talk about gambling, betting on anything?"

"If he did I never paid no attention to it. Course, he might be like a lot of fellas. Play the numbers just like they was breathing, but they never say nothing about it until they hit or until they miss by one number and then you hear 'em bitching."

Balzic nodded. "You ever see the fat guy before?"

"Never."

"Ever see anybody who looked like him, built the same way, only a little taller and a couple years older?"

"Nope."

"Well, is there anything else you can remember about Dulia, anything at all?"

Harsha shook his head. "No. I didn't have much to do with him. I keep pretty much to myself. Ever since my missus died, I don't feel like socializing too much, if you know what I mean. No, until he starts getting this screwy idea that his property goes ten feet more than it does, we never did nothing but pass the time of day. I never even drunk a beer with him."

"Was he a drinker?"

"Well, till he hurt his back, all I ever seen him drink was a couple beers after work when it was hot. But now he drinks a lot. Sweet wine. Buys it by the gallon, least twice a week. I heard him say once it was the only thing made his back quit hurting. Sounded to me like he was trying to kid somebody. But maybe it did. I been pretty lucky. I never had no back trouble, but I seen a lot of guys with it and they ain't worth a fart for working, so it must hurt. But that's all I know about him drinking."

"What about his family, his relatives?"

"Well, I think I already told you they didn't have no kids. Only relatives I ever seen visiting them was an old lady and her son and daughter. The daughter looked a mess. The only reason I even knew they was relatives at all was his missus told me, 'cause she felt sorry for the old lady on account of the daughter. But I don't even know their name. All I know was they was on his side of the family. But how they was related, hell, I don't even know that."

"The daughter was a mess? How do you mean?"

"Oh, I don't know, she just looked all lumpy, like a pile of putty. And Dulia, he used to look out for her. Every time they come, he used to follow her around their backyard like he was trying to make sure she didn't mess around with nothing, or maybe he was trying to make sure she didn't hurt herself. That's the way it looked to me."

Balzic thought a moment. Something struck him, some connection. He didn't know what it was, but he knew he knew what it was without being able to think of it clearly.

Balzic took out his notebook and asked for Harsha's address and phone number. Harsha gave his address but said, "I don't have no phone. I had them take it out after my missus died . . . hey, I been meaning to ask you. I mean, I guess you know what you're doing, but how's come this is the first thing you wrote down? All them detective shows I see on TV, them cops are always writing things down, making notes and all, when they're getting stories from witnesses, I mean."

Balzic smiled. "Andy, I was just about to tell you to come down the station so a stenographer could take your story in shorthand. She wouldn't miss a word, and if I was writing things down I wouldn't be able to read it tomorrow. Anyway, we have to notarize your statement and then we have to take it to a magistrate to file an information against this fat guy; otherwise you'd have to appear before a magistrate yourself, and there's no point in you doing that."

"Oh. I don't know what all that means, but I guess you know what you're doing."

"Well, don't worry about it. The thing is, I won't be able to get a stenographer until late tomorrow afternoon. Can you come in around four?"

"I could get there by about ten after, how's that?"

"That's fine. In the meantime, don't die on me—"

"Oh, hell, I'm healthy as a horse."

Balzic laughed. "I can see that. What's really important is that you don't forget anything you saw."

"Oh, shoot, I couldn't forget none of this, no sirree."

"Good. Then go on home and have a couple cold ones. And listen, if I'm not there tomorrow, just tell the desk sergeant what you're there for and he'll take care of you, okay?"

Harsha nodded and left with a shrug and a wave.

Balzic then called Stramsky at the station and told him to put out the word that Manditti was now wanted for attempted murder. "There's no question the dummy did it, Vic. He just beat the hell out of a guy named Francis Dulia with a baseball bat. Call Muscotti and tell him he better tell his people to get off their asses. Tell everybody to get off their asses. Something tells me Tullio ain't finished yet. I don't know why I got that feeling, but I do. In the meantime, I'm going to stay here and try to talk to Dulia's wife and Fat Manny."

A FIX LIKE THIS

* * *

Dulia's wife was still deep under the influence of the Nembutal, so Balzic went up to the third floor to see Fat Manny. He found him flat on his back gnawing on a stick of pepperoni, licking his fingers between bites.

"Hello, Manny. How you feeling?"

"I'm going to live. You feeling okay, Balzic? You going to live?"

"For a while I think."

"Good. We wouldn't know how to act around Rocks-burg if you wasn't the chief of police. You keep the streets safe and everything. Us citizens are really grateful."

Balzic saw that the other beds were still empty. He turned around and closed the door quietly. "Okay, Manny, let's cut the happy horseshit."

"What happy stuff? Am I giving you happy stuff? I thought we was just being nice."

"So okay, so keep on being nice and tell me why you screwed Francis Dulia."

"Huh? Who? Who was that again?"

"You never heard of him, huh?"

"Never heard of him," Manny said ponderously.

"Then why do you suppose your brother would want to put a job on him with a Louisville Slugger?"

"What're you talking about? What job? What slugger? My brother? You must be eating wrong, Balzic. You must be eating too much American bread or something. That stuff messes up your system. My brother would not even hurt a stray cat."

"Manny, I got everybody looking for him. Everybody on my force, plus all of Dom's people, plus state people, plus county people. Your brother's up for attempted murder. And even if Dulia doesn't die, which is unlikely considering that his skull is fractured in two places, not to mention a dozen other fractures—even if Dulia doesn't die, your brother's going away on every assault rap the state ever wrote. And as pissed off as Dom is at you, you have to know that Tullio's going to go it alone. He won't get any of the fringe benefits, not so much as an extra pack of cigarettes a week."

Manny took another bite of pepperoni and chewed it slowly, thoughtfully, but he said nothing.

"I mean, think of it, Manny. When we get him there isn't going to be anybody standing up for him. He's going to go up in front of the man all by himself, and then he's going to do all that time by himself. And he won't do it at the hotel down the road, Manny. He'll be doing it in Pittsburgh, in The Wall, where they keep the bad guys, the crazies. And not a friend, inside or out. So why don't you give your brother a break and tell me where he's going? He turns himself in and maybe he won't have to go to Pittsburgh. Maybe he'll find out he has some friends."

"That don't make no sense, Balzic. I mean, even if I knew what you were talking about, and even if I knew where he was going—hell, who says he's going anywhere? He's probably home. Besides, how could he turn himself in if you had to go get him? And what's he going to turn himself in for anyway? He ain't done nothing."

"You just tell me where he is, Manny, I'll call him on the phone. You let me talk to him for five minutes, I guarantee he'll be begging me to let him turn it over. You know there's about ninety percent spades down there? Do I have to tell you how your brother likes spades?"

"Balzic, you're trying to pump carbon monoxide up somebody's ass, that's what you're trying to do. I don't know what you're talking about."

"You don't know any Francis Dulia?"

"How many times I got to tell you?"

"And you never booked a winner for him and then told him to take a walk?"

"I don't know where you're getting this stuff. I don't book nothing. I'm a chauffeur, everybody knows that."

"Who're you trying to shit? You haven't driven anything anywhere for anybody for over a week. How'd you get those holes in you?"

Manny thought for a moment. "It happened like this. I was carrying a bunch of quart pop bottles in a bag. I was gonna take them back for the deposit. The bag broke and one of them fell out the bottom and I tripped on it. Then I fell down on top of the rest of them. They broke. I mean, I'm pretty heavy, you know?"

"Oh, Jesus, Manny, that's enough. I'm going to ask you just once more not to be dumb. What do you say?"

Manny rolled over on his side, grimacing and wheezing, the bed creaking ominously. He laid the stick of pepperoni on his nightstand. "Hey, Balzic, there's some olives and bread underneath there. You wanna hand it to me, huh?"

"You tell me where Tullio is, I'll go get you a banquet."

"Aw fuck you. I'll call a nurse. Who needs you?"

"I think you and your brother are both going to need me pretty bad before this is over. But with all the static you're giving me, maybe I won't be around."

"Hey, Balzic, all of a sudden I'm tired. I don't want no more conversation. I think I need my rest."

Balzic snorted. "I wish you'd give me a rest. Right now I'm wondering how Tullio's going to take it when I tell him what kind of diet you're trying to put him on. After all the food he brought you in here? And you're not going to be able to take him a pepperoni."

"See you around, Balzic. I'm asleep."

"Have it your way, fatso. You just better start praying that Dulia doesn't die."

"Everybody dies, Balzic. And don't call me fatso. Fat Manny, that's okay. But I don't go for that fatso stuff."

"Just what're you going to do about it, fatso?" Balzic snarled. "Laying there with your lard full of holes, just what do you think you can do about it? Go call your fatso brother and tell him to put a job on me with his bat? I wish you would. And I wish he would. 'Cause I'm so pissed at you two fat-asses, I'd like nothing better than to have him coming at me with a bat. I keep a three-foot baton in my car, fatso. Your fatso brother ever comes at me with a bat, I'll show him some moves with that baton he won't believe. You hear me, fatso?"

"Blow it out your ass, Balzic. You're giving me a headache."

Balzic turned and left, muttering and cursing under his breath. Once out in the hall, he stopped and faced the wall, making his hands into fists, chewing his lips, and fighting the urge to knock holes in the plaster. The way I'm going, he thought, it'd be my luck to hit a stud. That's all I'd need. My hand in a cast. . . .

He shoved his hands into his pockets and went to the elevators, taking one to ground level, then walking quickly to the Emergency Unit. He found Mrs. Kwalick and had her direct him to the room where Mrs. Dulia was. It was a waste of time; Mrs. Dulia woke in wild-eyes starts only to doze off in midreply to one of his questions. Nothing she managed to blurt out was of any use to him.

Balzic paced around the room for some minutes trying to think if there was something he should be doing that he had forgotten or overlooked, but the more he paced and looked at his watch, the more he knew that the only thing he could do was wait and hope for some good luck. Maybe I ought to get

A FIX LIKE THIS

somebody praying, he thought, and went out to the pay phone in the lobby. He dialed St. Malachy's rectory.

Father Marrazo answered gruffly.

"This is Mario, Father. How you doing?"

"The same," the priest said in Italian.

"You having any luck with your problem?"

"You mean about Father Sabatine?"

"Yeah."

"It's going to take more than luck, Mario."

Balzic waited for him to go on, but the priest said nothing. "Well, uh, how 'bout praying? Isn't that helping?"

"Mario, I hope you never hear me say anything like this again, but I'm nearly prayed out. The bishop is so angry he can't talk, and Sabatine is so depressed he won't talk. And I'm getting ready to dump the whole thing on Kelly and Marcellino."

"Oh." Balzic didn't know what else to say.

"Was there something you wanted, Mario?"

"Huh? Oh, no. No, I just wanted to see how you were making out with your problem, that's all."

"Well, what can I tell you?"

"Nothing—I guess. Sorry to bother you. I hope you, uh, I hope it works out." Balzic hung up without saying good-by. Well, he thought, no help there. Not even a little shot of consolation. But there's no use getting worked up about it. He has his own problems. I can't expect him to do my work. Probably wouldn't have done any good anyway to have him praying, but it sure would have made things feel better. "My ass," Balzic said aloud, as he turned away from the phone and looked around. "My ass. . . ."

"Such language," said an old woman with hair so gray it was turning yellow. She was sitting on an imitation leather couch beside the phone. In front of her was a four-legged aluminum walker. She clucked her tongue at Balzic. "What would your mother say?" she said sharply.

Balzic stared down at the woman, but he could not bring himself to tell her that if his mother had been there she would have told the old woman to mind her own business and stay out of other people's conversations.

"Young man," the woman snapped, "if you don't leave me alone, I'm going to call the police." Her eyes were as hard as the set of her mouth.

"Old woman," Balzic said, "I am the police. And right now there's nothing I'd rather do than leave you alone. Good afternoon."

The old woman's face softened suddenly in a crooked smile. "It was so nice of you to bring me here," she cooed. "The people are all so wonderful. Have you met my son?"

"No, ma'am," Balzic said, recognizing at last the woman's senility. "No, ma'am, I haven't."

Her face pinched as she squinted meanly at Balzic. "You should," she hissed. "He's a bastard just like you."

Balzic shook his head and walked away from her. He stopped in the center of the lobby and looked around. Every seat was occupied. He turned slowly and looked at each of the faces, seeing on one confusion, on another irritation, on still another impatience, on still another grim-lipped pain. There was a woman, enormously pregnant, with her ankles and feet so swollen that she had taken off her slippers and stockings and was staring glumly at her feet. There was a teenaged boy with a blood-soaked hanky wrapped around his hand. There was an old man, his nostrils half destroyed by cancer, who was staring blankly at his hands. A black woman, her face stony, was trying half-heartedly to soothe a young girl who would not stop crying though outwardly nothing appeared to be wrong with her. There

A FIX LIKE THIS

was another old man, breathing in phlegmatic bursts, who was turning an unlit cigarette over and over in his fingers. There was a young woman with long, frizzy red hair and very fair skin who sat with her chin in her hand. She seemed to be talking to herself, and when Balzic looked at her, she jumped up suddenly and hurried past him toward the exit, saying to herself, "Fuck this place. I mean, this place can just go fuck." And then she was gone.

Balzic could not look at the rest of the faces. He felt suddenly that if he didn't get out of there, if he didn't get outside into the crisp March air, he was going to choke on the confusion and irritation and impatience and pain. He stood transfixed for a moment and then wheeled about and nearly ran out of the lobby.

Outside, he gulped air and loosened his tie and wanted to untie his shoes and undo his belt. He tried to remember when he had felt such an overpowering sense of oppression. Then he asked himself what the point was of trying to remember that. A comparison was senseless. Besides, he thought, what the hell do you expect to see in an emergency waiting room? That's the way it looks every day of the week. And on the holidays? When the solid citizens are out having fun? Hell, man, today that place was practically healthy.

It was eleven-thirty-two in the evening when Balzic got the phone call from the hospital. He had never met the doctor and had to ask him twice to repeat his name. Even then he wasn't sure he could pronounce it. The doctor was another Lebanese.

"Not that it matters all that much," Balzic said, "but when did he die?"

"Eleven-twenty," the doctor said. "I just completed the death certificate."

"Did he ever regain consciousness?"

"No."

"What did you put down as the cause of death?"

"Massive brain damage as a direct result of multiple fractures of the left parietal and left temporal bones."

"Is Dr. Grimes there?"

"Not now, no. He had the body removed immediately to the morgue. I am sure he will have a full report for you in the morning."

"How's Dulia's wife taking it?"

"I'm told she is quite incoherent."

"Well that's natural, I guess. Thank you." Balzic hung up and stared at the phone. He scratched the back of his left hand and thought for a long moment, his eyes wide and unblinking.

"Hey, Vic," he said, looking up to see Stramsky looking back at him expectantly.

"It's murder now, right?" Stramsky said.

Balzic nodded. "Poor sonofabitch never woke up . . . it was probably better." Balzic stood and went to the window overlooking Main Street. He jingled coins and keys in his pockets and listened vaguely to Stramsky calling all units and personnel to change the charge on Tullio Manditti to a general charge of murder. Stramsky then called the state police and told them that the investigation was now officially theirs.

There were only a few cars moving on Main Street and no pedestrians that Balzic could see. The temperature had dropped fifteen degrees since the afternoon, and Balzic fully expected to see snow. Wind lifted bits of paper from the gutters and off the sidewalks and swirled them about, but there was no snow. He watched the paper being blown this way and that, and he found himself thinking that his mind was working the same way: bits of information were coming and going with little apparent sense.

A FIX LIKE THIS

It should have been a simple matter. Manny had booked a winner on his own for Francis Dulia, and when Manny couldn't come up with the money Dulia went berserk. That was logical enough. One guy with an appetite bigger than his brain hustles a guy with a bad back, an unemployed guy who lately was given to moods of surly indignation. Nothing to it. Enter the brother with his bat, exit one guy who thought the world was out to screw him and found out that he was right. What could be more logical than that?

But what was Dulia telling Tullio during that couple of minutes before Tullio straightened up and said he was going to beat his brains out? Tullio didn't go there to kill him. You don't put a towel around the bat if you're looking to kill him. The towel's there to keep from killing him. And Tullio never hit him in the head until after Dulia quit making his speech—whatever it was.

Then there was that thing Dulia said. "It couldn't lose. It wasn't supposed to lose." That's what Harsha said he said, and Harsha had absolutely no doubt about it. "It wasn't supposed to lose." ... Ah, that's crap. There isn't a bettor in the world who thinks he's booking a loser. Still, this wasn't the ordinary bettor. This guy was ballsy enough to try to collect his winnings with a knife.

So what the hell did he bet on? It had to be a number. That's the only bets Manny ever carried. But how does this guy think a number couldn't lose? Old stock, new stock, New York race, Brooklyn race—that's all the numbers there are. The stocks come out of *The Wall Street Journal* and the races come out of the *The New York Daily News* ... every guy who ever tried to fix one of those numbers got dead in a real hurry. And this Dulia, this square from Westfield Township? Who the hell could he know to even begin to fix anything?

So why am I thinking fix? Good question. Why am I? Because it doesn't make sense for a guy who's about to lose his life to say something like that? Okay. So what would he be saying? Oh, shit, I don't know what all he said to Tullio. Just that.

No, goddamn it. He said that because he was sure, that's why. Because he was right. That was a guy looking for what was his, what belonged to him, what was owed. Maybe they weren't much—what the hell is ten feet of property more or less? But if you've hurt your back and you can't work and you feel like the world has just given you the shaft, you start making sure you get what you think is really yours. That was a guy with a grudge against the world, and he was looking for sure things. A guy getting ready to die who cares more that what he bet on wasn't supposed to lose—he cares more about that than he does about living or dying. That guy had to know something. He knew a fix was in. Some kind of fix. Had to be. . . .

Balzic reached for a phone and dialed.

"Yes?" Dom Muscotti answered curtly.

"This is Mario. Dulia died."

Muscotti made growling noises. "That's—that's a shame. A friggin' shame. I'm sorry, Mario, I really am."

"Are you sure you didn't know him, Dom?"

"Sure I'm sure. I told you before when you called. I thought then that I maybe heard the name someplace, but now I'm sure I didn't." Dom paused. "That friggin' Tullio, wait'll I . . ." His voice trailed off.

"Wait'll what?"

"Nothing, Mario. Did I say something?"

"Skip it," Balzic said, sighing impatiently. "You sure this guy didn't book with one of your people?"

"Mario, I asked everybody, honest. Listen, what would I be lying for now?"

"Keep your shirt on. I didn't say you were lying."

"Well, nobody knows him, I'm telling you."

"D'you talk to Manny yet?"

"Not yet. I'm going up the hospital as soon as I close up. I don't know what the occasion is, but I got a bunch of college hot dogs in here and they're celebrating something. I'd've closed up an hour ago if it wasn't for them, but I need the paper."

"You need the paper?" Balzic laughed.

"What're you laughing for? You think I don't take a beating every once in a while? I'll write you a letter. There's some guy killing me. I think he must have something on a couple jockeys or something. Christ, I can't handle him no more this week. I laid him off yesterday to Pittsburgh and today to Buffalo. What do you think that's gonna cost me?"

"I don't want to know," Balzic said. "Well, tell your people it's murder now. And when you talk to Manny, tell him I'm making him an accessory before and after. Conspiracy, the whole bit."

"I'll tell him," Muscotti said. "Don't worry about nothing. I'm gonna talk to him like a father."

Balzic hung up and thought it over. If Muscotti did know Dulia, why would he say he didn't? To protect Manny? Not likely. Muscotti was sore enough a week ago at Manny to give him a vacation despite his own mother's fondness for Manny's company and conversation, and there was no one alive Muscotti tried to please as much as his mother.

What's more, it had been sixteen years since Muscotti had used muscle for anything. Since Sam Weisberg retired to Florida, there had been no reason to use muscle. Muscotti was solid with the old men in Pittsburgh, and nobody would dare provoke him without provoking them.

Balzic could only conclude that Muscotti was telling the truth: neither he nor any of his people knew Dulia, professionally or otherwise.

So what the hell did Dulia fix? Balzic drummed his fingers on the desk and began to think that there was a good chance he was complicating a simple thing.

He shook his head. There was still Dulia's life-and-death insistence that what he had bet on couldn't lose, and try as he might, Balzic could not put that thought out of his mind. He kept rattling it around, thinking that there was something right in front of him that he was overlooking, something everybody took for granted which he just couldn't connect to Dulia. He was sure it had to be something local. Dulia couldn't be anything but a local square who tried to make a local score.

At five to twelve Sergeant Joe Royer came in and took over the desk from Stramsky. The rest of the shift changed, and everybody brought in the same word: no Tullio.

By one that morning, Balzic had decided that Dulia had been a square, a dumb square who had stumbled onto something.

By one-thirty, Balzic had decided that Dulia had been the most cunning man in the county.

By two o'clock, Balzic admitted that he didn't know a damned thing about Francis Dulia.

He called Romeo's Diner and ordered a cheeseburger. When it was delivered, he took two bites out of it and wrapped the rest of it up and put it in his desk. His tongue was biting from all the cigarettes, his throat and chest were burning, and his stomach was growling from all the coffee.

He drew oblong boxes on a note pad, filling them in until they were solidly black, then drew some more and filled those in. Dozens of questions about Dulia rumbled through his mind, and he fumed that he couldn't get answers to any of them until the workmen's compensation bureau opened in the morning. He'd have to work backward from there, and with any luck, he might know something about Dulia by noon. Until then, all he knew was that he was trying to grab a handful of smoke by even thinking about Dulia until he had some pertinent details about the man's life.

At two-twenty-five the phone rang, and Balzic lurched to answer it.

"Hey, kiddo," his mother said, her voice hoarse, "how come you no come home?"

"Huh? Ma? What're you doing still up?"

"Aw, my ankles hurt. They wake me up. But never mind. How come you no come home, no call or nothing? Ruth li'l bit worried, kiddo. She li'l bit mad too. You should call at least."

"I know, Ma, I know. I'm sorry."

"Better make up with Ruth tomorrow. Not me. Tell her you sorry."

"Okay, Ma, I will. Now go back to bed, okay? Try to get some sleep."

"Oh, Mario, sometime I don't mind I can't sleep. Sometime I just like sit here by myself. I take some wine, and I think about long time ago."

"Well, don't think too much. You can't get it back, that's what you're always telling me."

"Sure, I know that. But I don't feel sad about the long time ago. I just like to think about, that's all."

"Okay. Well, good night, Ma. I don't want to talk much right now, okay?"

"Hey, wait, kiddo. Is you—you stay late because of Frankie Dulia?"

Balzic frowned at the receiver as though it were responsible for what he'd just heard. "Yeah, Ma. But how'd you know about that?"

"Oh, I talk with Rose today. She feel very bad."

"Rose who?"

"Oh, Mario, what's wrong with your memory all of a sudden? Rose Abbatta, that's Rose who."

"Mrs. Abbatta told you about him?"

"Yeah, sure. Didn't I just say?"

"Yeah, but how'd she know about him?"

"Mario, he's her nephew."

Balzic straightened his back. "Say that again, Ma?"

"What'sa matter with you, you drunk? Frankie Dulia is Rose Abbatta's nephew."

"No I'm not drunk. Just tell me how Mrs. Abbatta found out what happened."

"Well, Nicky, he buys Rosalie a bicycle couple days ago, last week sometime, and right away she want to take over to show Frankie. But Rose don't let her until today. So Rosalie go over, but nobody's home. So the neighbor man, he tell Rosalie Frankie's in the hospital, got all beat up. And Rosalie come home all crying and wet her pants and, oh, was just carry on terrible. Rose said it took her half-hour to get Rosalie calm down so she can say what's happen. Rosalie really love Frankie a lot. Ever since they was kids, he look out for her, and—"

"Ma, I should've known. I should've known," Balzic said, shaking his head and thumping the desk with the side of his fist.

"You shoulda know what?"

"I should've known to call you in the first place."

"Hey, I call you, kiddo, you forget?"

"It doesn't make any difference, Ma. I got to hang up now. Don't worry. Go to sleep. And thanks."

"For what?"

"I got to go, Ma, honest. I can't talk anymore now. Wait a minute. What's Mrs. Abbatta's address?"

"Huh? What you want that for?"

"Please, Ma, just give it to me, okay?"

"Okay, okay. She live on Pinewood Drive. In Westfield Township. I don't remember number. But she's live in third house on right-hand side."

"From which end?"

"From this end. From when you go out from town."

"Oh thank you, Mother. You're beautiful. G'night."

"Hey—"

Balzic cut her off, held his finger on the receiver button, and waved to Royer to come over. He lifted his finger and dialed the operator and then scribbled a note for Royer. Royer looked at it, puzzled, and held up his hands questioningly.

"Tell somebody to get down there and pick him up," Balzic said.

"What charge?"

"Make one up. But tell them to move it. Operator? Operator, this is the Rocksburg police. This is an emergency. I want you to get the residence of a Mrs. Rose Abbatta on Pinewood Drive in Westfield Township. The number may be listed under her son's name. Nicholas or Nicolao. And keep ringing until somebody answers."

The operator said she would and clicked off. There was a long pause. Then the operator came back on. "Sir, that line is busy. If this is an emergency, do you authorize me to interrupt that call?"

"Hell yes. Cut in on it!"

Balzic looked up at the clock above the radio console. "I hope you worked overtime tonight, buddy," he said aloud. "Of all nights, I hope you got some time and again tonight...."

The shriek ripped into Balzic's ear and set his flesh tingling. He thrust the phone outward and then brought it slowly closer to his ear until he could hear without being hurt by the pitiful but piercing cries of Mrs. Abbatta.

"Please send ambulance! Please, God, my Nicky is hurt! Please, please send ambulance quick!"

Balzic shouted to Royer, "Forget that last thing I told you. Get Mutual Aid and send them over to Pinewood Drive in Westfield Township—hold it till I get the address.

"Mrs. Abbatta, this is Mario Balzic. Listen to me. What's your house number? Mrs. Abbatta, do you hear me?"

She would not stop. She kept calling, pleading, for somebody to help her help her son.

"Mrs. Abbatta, goddamnit, I am trying to help you. This is Mario Balzic. Stop yelling a minute and tell me your house number!"

She sucked in her breath and then coughed violently. It took her nearly a minute to stop and control her voice. "God forgive me," she said. "Mario, I know your mother all my life . . . God forgive me."

"Mrs. Abbatta, never mind about God right now, okay? Just tell me your house number."

"It's all my fault, oh, God," she whispered. Then she sobbed and fought the sob so that she sounded as though she were being strangled. Finally she blurted out, "Number fifteen. Fifteen, you hear?"

"I hear. Fifteen." Balzic called it out loud enough for Royer to hear. And then he repeated the address so there could be no mistake. "Okay, Mrs. Abbatta, you go be with Nick now. There's an ambulance on the way right now. You hear me? Mrs. Abbatta, you hear me?"

"Yes, yes, I hear."

"I'm going to hang up now, Mrs. Abbatta. You just go stay with your son. People will be there to help him in just a few minutes, you hear?"

"Yes, I hear. Thanks God. Oh, thanks God. . . ."

"Good. Just go be with him." Balzic depressed the receiver button, lifted it, and dialed Troop A barracks of the state police, asking for the duty officer.

"Lieutenant Poli," a voice said after a moment.

"This is Balzic in Rocksburg, Poli. I need a couple mobiles real quick."

"No kidding. Do you now?"

"Cut the crap, Poli. We got one murder tonight and we may have another possible. Same suspect, and he's got to be in the area. I need—"

"Balzic, I can't help what you need. I got three people down with the flu. I was told to assign you one unit, and that's the one you got cruising Norwood Hill. In the morning you're supposed to get another one. I couldn't give you another one if I wanted to because I don't have one to give."

"Okay, Poli, thanks anyway." Balzic hung up and pushed the cuticle back on his thumb, calling out to Royer, "Tell all the mobiles to concentrate on the area between Westfield Township and Norwood. I'm betting a thousand to one that fat-ass is just going to go on home and make out like nothing's happening. That would be his style."

Royer sent out the message and then said, "She was calling Mutual Aid when you cut in."

"Huh? Who?"

"That woman, Abbatta. She was trying to call them herself. The Mutual Aid dispatcher said to thank you. He couldn't get her house number out of her until you cut in."

"Oh. Big fuckin' deal. I did something right."

"Hey, uh, Mario, what's going on? I mean, how'd you know to call that place? And what did you want this Nick Abbatta picked up for down at the paper?"

"Oh, Joe, Jesus Christ, it's a long story. A long, messy story. But to make it quick, it has to do with a lottery. You know the kind I'm talking about. Everybody with a building fund or a mortgage or some fuckin' charity for some guy who broke his leg playing softball runs them. The American Legion, the VFW, the Moose, the Sons of Italy, the Polish Falcons, the Kosciusko Club, the Russian Club, the churches, all those phony athletic clubs, the Amvets, Christ, you name 'em, they've all run them at one time or another. Most of them run off the stock numbers, but lately a lot them are picking the winner from the last three digits of the U.S. Treasury balance . . . hell, I got two in my wallet right now. One from the VFW and another one from the Polish Falcons Stramsky sold me."

"Yeah, okay," Royer said. "I got one from Stramsky myself. But I still don't get it. How'd you know to call that house? I mean, I can't figure what the hell happened up there."

"Tullio got to him, that's what happened," Balzic said, standing and stretching and letting out a long, disgusted sigh that sounded more like a snarl, "What a fuckin' stupid I am. Right under my face. I knew there was a fix, I just fuckin' knew it! But you think I could put it together? Goddamn! . . . I also knew it was a pile of crud, but I never thought it was going to be this big a pile . . . oh, Jesus, Mary, and Joseph, wait'll the newspapers and TV guys get hold of this—well, at least there's going to be one newspaper that ain't going to be playing it on the front page."

"Mario, I must've left my head out in the car," Royer said, "but I still don't know what you're talking about."

Balzic walked toward the door. He was in no hurry. He knew it was only a matter of time before they got Tullio, and he knew Tullio was finished. Right now he was probably burying his bat or sawing it in little pieces and burning it. "You just think about it some more, Joe. I'm sure you'll put it together. In the meantime, stay on the horn. I want everybody awake out there. That fat-ass can't have gone too far. I'm going up the hospital, see if there's anything I can do for Mrs. Abbatta."

Balzic didn't use his light or his siren to get to the hospital. Because he passed only three other cars, he didn't have to use them. But he wouldn't have used them anyway, not even if he had been in five o'clock traffic. He was feeling so stupid he didn't want anybody to know he was a cop. They'd all bust a gut, he thought. If they knew how much I didn't know, they'd all crawl into caves and get themselves some rocks . . . aw fuck this. What the hell am I thinking about? Christ, if you don't know the relations, you don't know anything. You got to know who relates to who, 'cause until you do, you're as dumb as the day you were born. You got to know who knows who, who has what, who wants what, who can do which for how much—you got to know that or you can sit around all day long picking fuzz out of your bellybutton. . . .

The Emergency Unit waiting room was improbably quiet when Balzic walked in. He had thought an ambulance would have had sufficient time to bring Nick Abbatta in, but he saw in a glance that there was only one person in the room. A middle-aged black man, thin as sticks, sat slumped in the corner of the couch nearest the fire doors leading into the treatment rooms. There was a large swelling above his left eye, his right eye was puffed nearly closed, and his lower lip was split so badly that it looked like beef liver. He was trying to smoke a cigarette, but the paper kept sticking to his lip and he was cursing under his breath about it.

Balzic walked directly to the admissions desk but found no one there. In an adjoining office to the rear he could hear someone talking on a phone. He started to go into the treatment rooms, but stopped when he felt the presence of someone close behind him. It was the black man.

"Ain't you the chief of police?"

"That's right. Something I can do for you?"

"I think maybe you better arrest me or somethin'."

"Oh yeah? Why should I do that?"

"'Cause I just beat the motherfuck outta my woman."

Balzic sighed, wanting to say, not right now, don't bother me, some other time maybe, right now I got enough people getting worked over, but he didn't. He said, "Is she here? Is she trying to file a complaint against you?"

"Naw, she ain't here. She at her place," the black man said. "And I don't know if she goin' file no complaint. All I know is I come on over her place and she don't say two words, she jus' start into bangin' on me with a skillet. She like to tore my head off."

"And then you beat her up, right?"

"Not jus' then. I wait till she asleep. Then I beat the motherfuck outta her."

"Oh, Christ," Balzic said. "How do you know you didn't kill her?"

"Oh I ain't killed her. She was still runnin' her motor mouth when I walked out the house."

"So you think that means she's still alive, huh?"

"Well I ain't never heard no dead person talk, has you?"

"Why the hell did you have to pick tonight?" Balzic said. He was sorry immediately after he'd said it.

"Hey, man, all I'm doin' is tellin' you. You don't wanna do nothin' 'bout it, that's cool with me. That's jus' fine with me. I'll jus' go on back over there and sit down and wait some more till they gets ready to stitch up my lip."

"You know what? That's a good idea. If she files a complaint against you, then I'll be happy to arrest you, how's that?"

"That's fine with me," the black man said, turning away to take a seat again. He took a couple of steps and then turned back. "Say, man, you wouldn't happen to have no cigarette with a cork filter on it. This paper keep messin' over my lip."

"There's a cigarette machine around the corner down that hall," Balzic said, pointing to the hall behind the man's back, but he recognized from the man's expression that he had no money. Balzic rooted in his pockets and found enough change for the man to buy a pack. The man took the money with his eyes downcast.

"I'll pay you this back in the mornin'," he said.

"Forget it. Pay me back by not beating your wife anymore."

"Oh, she ain't my wife. I learned long time 'go, you don't marry no woman. You marry a woman, you wrong with the law right from the go. She can put you out, put you in jail, put you in a mental institution, take your money, take your clothes, your car—she can jus' get over you somethin' terrible. And there ain't a motherfuck you can do 'bout it." The man set off toward the cigarette machine, shaking his head, and saying repeatedly, "She ain't my wife. Ain't no woman my wife. My momma didn't raise no fool. . . ."

Balzic heard the commotion outside then but didn't even bother going to the door because he knew that the ambulance crew knew its business and that the best thing he could do was stand clear.

The attendants, hunched over and scurrying the stretcher along, bumped through the outer swinging doors and past Balzic and then through the fire doors, entering the treatment rooms.

One quick look at Nick Abbatta's face was enough for Balzic. If Abbatta was alive at all, it was only because the paramedics in the ambulance crew had found some dim signal of life and were hurrying more out of duty and hope than sense.

Balzic felt himself going queazy in the stomach and cold across the chest. Then he saw Mrs. Abbatta herding her daughter

Rosalie through the outer doors. Rosalie was mumbling something inaudible over her shoulder to her mother, but Mrs. Abbatta paid no attention; instead she put both hands in the middle of Rosalie's back and shoved her forward. Rosalie stopped short at the sight of Balzic, and her mother cried out, "Go on, move, you, you stupid!"

Balzic walked quickly toward them and held out his arms to embrace Mrs. Abbatta. She fell into his arms and sobbed against his chest. Rosalie scooted clumsily out of the way and dropped onto a couch, bumping her legs against it. She put all four fingers of her right hand into her mouth and began to whimper.

"Shut up, you," Mrs. Abbatta snapped at her. "This my fault, God forgive me, but you—you stupid!"

"Easy, Mrs. Abbatta," Balzic said. "Easy."

"Oh, no," she said. "I can no be easy with her this time. All her life I be easy with her. But no, not this time. This time she should be in there. Not Nicky. Not my Nicky."

Balzic had no doubt that if he hadn't been holding her around the shoulders, she would have attacked her daughter. Rosalie sucked backward against the couch, one foot on top of the other, and she tried to get all the fingers of both hands into her mouth. Tears streamed down her plump cheeks and mucous bubbled from her nostrils.

Balzic tried to steer Mrs. Abbatta toward a chair, but she resisted him. "I want be with Nicky," she cried. She repeated it over and over, and Balzic had all he could do to keep her from tearing loose and rushing into the treatment rooms to find her son.

"Please sit down, Mrs. Abbatta. Please."

"What goods to sit? I got to do something."

"Mrs. Abbatta, believe me, you'll only be in the way in there. These people know what they're doing. They'll take care of Nicky." It was a kind lie to tell, but a lie nonetheless, and from the way Mrs. Abbatta looked at him, he could see that she knew he was just telling one of those kind lies. She glared at him fiercely for it, but then she seemed to droop. She covered her face with her hands and let Balzic ease her into an overstuffed chair.

She began to speak in Italian, but talking so low and quickly that Balzic could not follow her accurately. She sounded as though she was saying something about her daughter, about what a burden God had given her in this life, about how she had been able to stand it until now, but that this was too much. This was the last weight she could—or would—carry. From now on she was no longer going to take the responsibility for her daughter. It was her fault, God knew, but it was Rosalie's just as much.

Balzic wasn't positive about the first part of what she'd said, but he felt sure he'd understood her when she'd said that she was not going to be responsible for her daughter anymore and that it was Rosalie's fault as much as hers.

"Mrs. Abbatta, you can't mean what you're saying."

"About what?" she demanded suddenly in English. Her eyes flashed toward her daughter, still sucking her fingers and whimpering on the couch. "About her? Goddamn right I mean. As God my witness. If God forgive me for Nicky, then God forgive me for her too."

"Hey, what's goin' on? I was 'posed to be next." It was the black man back from the cigarette machine and looking outraged.

"You'll get your turn," Balzic said to him, at the same time putting his hand on Mrs. Abbatta's shoulder.

"Ain't this a bitch," the black man said. "This stuff always goin' on. Let a white man get in here and—"

"Sit down and shut up," Balzic said. "You don't have half an idea what's going on. Just find yourself a seat."

"Don't tell me find no seat! I can stand if I want. You can put me in the back the line, but I can damn sure stand if I wants. Huh!"

"I don't care if you hang from the ceiling," Balzic said, moving toward the man. "Just turn it off."

The black man grunted, turned and looked at Rosalie, and said to her matter of factly, "See how they do, girl? Onliest way it ever been. Black men and ugly women always gets in last."

Balzic wanted to knock him down, but in glancing at Rosalie, he saw that what the man had said had had a curiously calming effect on her. She took her fingers out of her mouth and wiped them on her robe. She sniffed and looked up at the black man as though wanting him to say more and as though it didn't matter much what he said.

The black man walked over and stood in front of Rosalie. "You better blow your nose, girl. We both know you a mess, but ain't no use you makin' a bigger mess." He walked off suddenly, disappearing behind the admissions desk, his head bobbing as he looked for something, and then returned carrying a box of tissues. He held them out to Rosalie and said, "Here, girl, clean up your face. You lookin' sorry as a Salvation Army suit."

Rosalie did not hesitate. She took the box of tissues, said "Thank you very much," and wiped her face and blew her nose. When she finished, she giggled up at the black man, her lumpy torso shaking with relief and gratitude.

Balzic turned back to Mrs. Abbatta, whose lips were stretched like wire across her teeth. "She how she does?" she whispered hoarsely. "Anybody treats her li'l bit nice, see how she does?" In Italian, she hissed the word for nigger. Then, still speaking Italian, she said, "Frankie was a nigger too."

Balzic went quickly to her side and sat on the arm of the chair. "What did you say?"

Again in Italian she said, "Frankie was the same. A nigger."

A FIX LIKE THIS

"Mrs. Abbatta, what're you talking about?"

"I'm the worst of everybody," she said, still speaking in Italian, but slowly and distinctly enough for Balzic to understand her clearly. "Nobody is worse than me. I made it come to this. If I had not agreed, it would never have come to this. So who am I to call names, to blame her or Frankie? Who am I to do this? I'm the real nigger in this."

Before Balzic could reply the ambulance crew came back out, and one of them motioned to Balzic that he wanted to talk to him. Balzic hurried to the man's side and listened with his head canted close to the man's mouth.

"I think somebody better get him a priest," the attendant whispered. "His heart's just fluttering."

Balzic cursed to himself as he went through his pockets looking for a dime. All he found were some pennies and one quarter. He went to the admissions desk, stepped behind it, and hit buttons on the phone there until he got a dial tone. Then he dialed St. Malachy's rectory.

Father Marrazo answered on the second ring, sounding as though he had been using wine to get to sleep and had succeeded only in getting a little drunk.

"This is Mario, Father. I'm at the hospital. They just brought in Nick Abbatta, and he needs you fast."

"Give me five minutes," the priest said. "Uh, Mario—never mind. I'll talk to you when I get there."

Balzic hung up, then ducked inside the treatment room doors and asked one of the nurses if the paramedic with the ambulance crew had been exaggerating. He got a somber, negative shrug in reply. He didn't know why he'd bothered to ask; he'd sensed as much when he'd seen Abbatta's face earlier.

He turned away slowly and walked as slowly back toward the doors leading to the waiting room, wanting to kick holes in the walls as he went. He came suddenly alert when he heard the scuffling in the waiting room.

He rushed out to find the black man hanging onto Mrs. Abbatta's left arm and trying to pull her away from her daughter. Mrs. Abbatta, old and portly though she was, kept leaning away from him, staying close enough to slap with her right hand at Rosalie's face but not getting close enough to connect. Rosalie had drawn herself into a corner of the couch and was shrieking wildly, begging her mother to stop.

Balzic darted around the black man and bear-hugged Mrs. Abbatta from behind, pinning her arms to her sides.

"For God's sake, Mrs. Abbatta, leave her alone. She's not responsible for this. Come on, leave her alone. Calm down."

"You think so, huh?" Mrs. Abbatta twisted herself, not to get free from Balzic but to look into his eyes. "Who you think tell Frankie? Her, that's who! This stupid!"

She sagged backward against Balzic and began to rock with sobs. "My God, my God . . . what did I do? . . ."

Balzic eased her across the width of the waiting room and gently pushed her down onto another couch. "Why don't you lay down for a while, Mrs. Abbatta? Really, try to lay down a little while."

She shook her head violently, then closed her eyes and pressed the heels of her palms against them. She began to speak very quietly between sobs. It took Balzic some moments to understand her Italian.

". . . I promise thee, O blessed Jude, to be ever mindful of this great favor, and I will never cease to honor thee as my special and powerful patron and to do all in my power to encourage devotion to thee. Amen. . . ." Then she began to say Hail Mary, finishing in a whisper.

Balzic had been squatting in front of her, holding her

shoulders, but he had to straighten up to shake the cramps out of his thighs.

Mrs. Abbatta began to pray again, this time in a voice almost less than a whisper, her hands still pressed tightly against her eyes. She finished just as Father Marrazo hurried into the waiting room, but she didn't look up to see who had come in.

The priest merely nodded at Balzic on his way through the lobby. In five minutes he was back out, shaking his head. His eyes were as near desperation as Balzic could ever recall seeing them.

Mrs. Abbatta took her hands away from her eyes, and instantly upon seeing the priest, she began to wail.

"Do you hear his confession?" she shrieked.

The priest nodded, but when Mrs. Abbatta cast her eyes downward in momentary relief, he shook his head no to Balzic.

"What can we do for her?" the priest asked after Mrs. Abbatta had cried and shouted for her son until she seemed unable to take another breath without collapsing.

"We can take them to my house," Balzic said. "My mother's really good at this." Balzic glanced over at Rosalie, who was still cringing on the couch. The black man was standing beside her, patting her on the head as he would have petted a puppy.

"The thing is," Balzic went on, taking the priest a few steps away, "she's really got the heat for her daughter. I can't take them alone, and neither can you, so she's going to have to sit up front with me and Rosalie can sit in the back with you; otherwise we're going to have one bitch of a time. We got to keep them apart until my mother can talk some sense into her—if that's possible."

"Well, let's do it," Father Marrazo said.

"Yeah, but I got to do something first." Balzic walked over to the black man and took his arm. The man cursed and tried to pull away, but Balzic wouldn't let go.

They went into the treatment rooms, where Balzic stopped the first nurse they came upon. "Will you see to it that this man is treated? He's been waiting a long time, and he's been damn good about it. And if he doesn't have any insurance, send the bill to the Rocksburg Police Department, you understand?"

Puzzled, the nurse nodded after a moment, then pointed to a room one door away and walked toward it, motioning for the black man to follow her. The black man scratched his head and then shook it, looking as though he couldn't think of anything to say and knowing that he would later regret that he hadn't been able to think of anything.

Balzic left him without another word, going back out to the lobby quickly. It took some persuading, both by him and by the priest, to convince Mrs. Abbatta that the best place for her to be now was with one of her best friends. She kept saying she wanted to be with Nicky, and then she tried to insist that she ought to be home. Together, Balzic and the priest got them into the cruiser, and Balzic drove to his house as fast as he thought he could without alarming either mother or daughter.

He didn't have to wake his mother; she had been sitting in the kitchen since she'd phoned him earlier. And when Balzic led them all into the kitchen she seemed instantly to sense what was wrong. She began immediately to soothe Mrs. Abbatta, asking nothing of anyone but reading all their faces.

Balzic relaxed then, knowing there was no one more capable of talking some sense into Mrs. Abbatta about Rosalie as soon as Mrs. Abbatta emptied herself of her next rush of grief. He also knew that before he closed the front door Ruth and the girls would be out to help. He and the priest got as far as the dining room when Ruth appeared.

"Mario, what the hell is going on?"
"In the kitchen. Mrs. Abbatta and Rosalie. Nick's dead."
"Oh my God, how?"
"I'll tell you later. Go help Ma, will you? I got to go."
"Oh for Christ's sake," she said and hurried into the kitchen without another word to her husband.

Balzic was checking the lock on his front door to make sure it would lock behind him when he heard his call signal crackling over the cruiser radio. He ducked around Father Marrazo and bounced down the steps two at a time.

"Balzic here. What's up, Joe?"

"Tullio's in his house, Mario," Desk Sergeant Joe Royer said.

"He's in his house? How the hell'd he get past those people up there? Never mind. I don't want to know. Is anybody talking to him?"

"Stramsky."

"Well tell him to tell everybody to sit on it. I'm on my way."

Balzic dropped the speaker on the seat, turned the ignition, and put the cruiser in gear. He looked out his window and saw the priest still standing on the steps. "What're you going to do, Anthony? Where you going? Your car's up the hospital. You can't do anything here. Come on, get in."

The priest shook his head thoughtfully, then trotted down the steps and around the front of the cruiser and got in. He had barely closed the door when Balzic stomped on the accelerator, throwing him against the dashboard.

"Easy, Mario, easy. I don't think he's going anywhere."

"Probably not. But I'm not hurrying because he might try to take off. I want to get there before one of my people decides to play the Lone Ranger."

Balzic made it to Norwood Hill, a distance of four miles, in less than three minutes. Father Marrazo was crossing himself when they got out.

All four of Balzic's mobile units were there with their spotlights trained on Manditti's house, as were one mobile from the state police and one from the county detectives, all of whom trailed after him as Balzic approached.

"What's the story, Vic?"

"Well, we got two in the back and two on each side, and the rest of us girls are where you see us."

"How long's he been in there?"

"The state guy signaled Fischetti about twenty minutes ago and he called me. After that it's all confusion. There's something wrong with the fuckin' radios again. Sometimes we can send and we can't receive, and then sometimes it's the other way around. My car radio's all fucked up too. Mario, you got to get some money from Council. We can't keep operating like this. Christ, somebody's—"

Balzic held up his hands. "I know all about the radios, Vic, but first things first, okay? Now, how'd he get in there?"

"He didn't drive in, that's for sure. He must've walked up over the back of the hill. It's a wonder he didn't have a heart attack."

"Who's been talking to him?"

"Just me. I don't know what the state horse said. I don't think anything."

"He said anything back?"

"Just once. He said for us to leave him alone before he got mad."

"Before he got mad, huh?"

Stramsky shrugged. "That's what he said, Mario."

"Okay, give me the horn."

Stramsky handed over the amplified bullhorn, and Balzic walked with it to the end of Manditti's front walk.

"Tullio? You hear me?"

A FIX LIKE THIS

No answer.

"Tullio, it's late, everybody's tired, we got half the hill up already, and the more noise I make on this thing, the more people we're going to wake up. There's lots of old people and babies up here need their sleep, so don't put any frost on my tomatoes, huh? Just get your butt out here. Now!" He turned to Stramsky and handed him the keys to his cruiser. "Go get the gas out of my trunk. I'm not gonna fuck around with this clown, not even for one minute."

A window squeaked open to the left of the front door.

"What're you, kiddin' me, Balzic?" came Tullio's voice from behind the window. "Whatta you want? What're you doing, screaming about old people and babies? What're you doing out there making all that racket and with them lights? You don't hear me making no noise. I ain't the one waking people up. So why don't you take them boy scouts and the rest of them fruitcakes and go on home? Cheesus."

"Tullio, for sure you're putting a frost on my tomatoes. I'm gonna tell you once more. If you're not out here in five seconds, you're gonna think you're in a gas factory."

Tullio let out a long groan and slammed the window shut. In four seconds he was standing in the doorway, shielding his eyes from the lights with his forearms.

"Turn them lights off, for crissake. What is this, Balzic? What're you doing this to me for? What'd I ever do to you, huh?"

"Just shut up and turn around and put your hands against the side of the house."

"Put my hands on the house, Cheesus. Turn them lights out so I can see what I'm doing."

"Go 'cuff him, Vic," Balzic said, "before I go up there and break his head."

Stramsky and the state trooper darted forward and

handcuffed and searched Tullio after they'd made him lean his forehead against the side of the house.

"Hurry up, willya?" Tullio kept shouting. "This hurts my head. I got a little weight here to hold up, you know."

"He's clean," Stramsky called back to Balzic, who was leaning against the fender of one of the cruisers. Father Marrazo stood next to him and started to pat his pockets, looking for cigarettes.

"There's some in my glove compartment, Father." Balzic faced the porch again. "Tell him his rights, Vic, and say 'em loud enough for the man from the state to hear."

Father Marrazo got the cigarettes from Balzic's car and began opening the pack in the spotlight from the cruiser Balzic was leaning against. Just then, Stramsky and the state trooper, each holding Tullio by an arm, led him down the walk and stopped in front of Balzic.

Tullio had come peacefully, if not quietly—he had never stopped complaining about the lights—but he took one look at Father Marrazo and went wild, screaming, cursing, kicking, lifting both Stramsky and the state trooper off the ground as he jerked his massive shoulders from side to side, all in a frenzied effort to get at the priest.

"You fuckin' priests! What're you doin' here? You fuckin' goddamn thieves! You're the biggest thieves! You got all them collection boxes, you ain't happy . . . you got to fix things, you motherfuckers!"

"Tap him!" Balzic called out to one of his own patrolmen who had just come from around the side of the house.

The patrolman drew his baton, scurried around the front of the frantic group, and when he'd taken aim, tapped Tullio on the forehead just hard enough to stun him and make him stop thrashing.

A FIX LIKE THIS

"Move again, Tullio," Balzic said, "and I'm going to take that baton and split your goddamn head open, you hear me?"

"I hear you, I hear you, Cheesus. What're you guys getting so rough for? I wasn't doing nothing."

"I'd hate to see you when you're doing something," Stramsky said, breathing heavily.

"I'm just looking out for my rights, that's all. That's all I'm doin' . . . us citizens got some rights, ain't that right, Balzic? . . . What's the priest doing here? Somebody getting married or something?" Tullio rattled on and on, but his jokes were only words.

There was no doubt now in Balzic's mind about who Tullio had really wanted to work over with his bat. Until this moment, until he had heard and seen Tullio's reaction to Father Marrazo's presence, Balzic had not been certain, but now he was absolutely sure. All he had to do was watch Tullio's eyes while he kept trying to make jokes. Tullio's gaze worked the priest over from head to foot and back up again.

It must have been a real struggle for him, Balzic thought, though it was hard to imagine Tullio ever struggling over a matter of conscience. Still, the situation had been the kind that would force even a Tullio into a struggle. Maybe for the first time in his life Tullio had had a real war in himself about who to get after he'd gotten Frank Dulia, and Balzic wondered how much had been added to that struggle by the thought of all those women . . . ah, it's all a lot of wasted wondering, Balzic concluded. I could ask him about it from now until I retire and he wouldn't tell me a thing.

"I want to see a lawyer, Balzic," Tullio said, his gaze still fixed on the priest.

"You'll get to see lots of them."

"You know what I mean," Tullio grumbled. "My own."

"Don't worry about it, Tullio. I'm sure Muscotti'll make sure you get the best lawyer he can get for you."

"Oh yeah," Tullio said disgustedly. "Write me a letter."

Balzic turned away and started for his own cruiser. "Book him, Vic. And no mistakes. I don't want to lose this clown over some bad bookkeeping."

Stramsky nodded, and he and the state trooper led Tullio off to the state mobile unit.

"Somebody put some locks on the house," Balzic called out to no one in particular. "I don't want to give these good people up here a chance to go bad on me . . . okay, let's go home. Let's everybody go home and think about what we're going to do with all that overtime, all that time and again. . . ."

In the cruiser, driving back to the hospital so Father Marrazo could get his car, Balzic said, "Okay, Father, are you going to tell me, or am I going to tell you?"

"Mario, if we both know, then what's the point? Any explaining either one of us has to do has to be to somebody else anyway."

"I don't know, Father. Maybe we ought to just clear the air with each other, you know?"

The priest shook his head slowly. "This is a real mess, Mario. No matter how much we talk about it, we still won't be able to change that."

"I know it's a mess. But what I can't get through my head is why Sabatine would go for something like this. I mean, sweet Jesus, rigging the Treasury balance—wow. I mean, I remember what you told me before about him. I didn't even know what you were talking about. I mean, I'm not sure I'd understand you now if you told me the same things all over again, but hell, Father, he had to be smarter than this."

"What can I tell you?" the priest said disconsolately. "He

did. For all I know it might have been his idea. I don't really know whose idea it was. Something tells me it was Mrs. Tuzzi's. But that's just a feeling. I can't get her to say anything about it, nothing at all. But no matter who approached who in the beginning, Sabatine could have stopped it any time he wanted, and he wouldn't have had to say a word."

"Well why the hell didn't he?" Balzic said, slapping the steering wheel repeatedly.

"You got a cigarette?"

"I thought you got the ones out of the glove compartment. Never mind. Here, take these," Balzic said, handing over a nearly crushed pack he had jammed behind the sun visor.

"There's only one left, Mario. I don't want to take your last one."

"I can get more in the hospital."

"So you want to give me this one?"

"What is this, Anthony? You got the ones from the glove compartment. What'd you do, lose 'em?" Balzic shot a quick glance at the priest. "Oh. Don't tell me. I can feel a homily coming on." Balzic waited, but the priest seemed content to smoke and stare out the window.

"Okay, Anthony, you got me hooked. What's the message?"

"It wasn't any big deal," the priest said. "You had something I seemed to need. We're friends. You gave it to me."

"You trying to tell me that's why Sabatine went for this?" Balzic screwed up his face and sighed. "Come on, Anthony. I don't know, but when I saw you a couple nights ago, before I knew any of this was connected, before I even had the first idea—damn, man, you made it sound a lot more complicated than that. A lot more complicated."

"It is a lot more complicated. But maybe when you cut all the details, maybe it was as simple as one person having something another person needed. You know, of all those women, only two of them had any kind of half-decent income? . . . You know where Mrs. Cafasso's son is? Domenico's widow—you know they only had one son—you know he's in the alcoholic ward in the Vets Hospital in Pittsburgh?"

"No, I didn't know that."

"He is. You know why? Because he was with Graves Registration at Normandy. He—"

"I know what they do, Anthony. They pick up the pieces and try to pair up the dog tags."

"That's not what I was going to say. I know you know what Graves Registration means. What I was going to say was that he hasn't been sober two days in a row since he was discharged. He got something like ninety percent disability, but he spent the whole check every month on booze. She never got a dime from him. And Domenico died of black lung before anybody thought of giving pensions for that . . . God, Mario, she was eating dog food. Imagine it! Dog food!

"And Mrs. Ruffola's story isn't much different," Father Marrazo continued. "Her husband went the same way, same disease. Their only son was killed at Salerno, about three miles from where both of them were born, her and Amadie. You know that Amadie refused to accept the insurance check from the government? He threw the guy who tried to deliver it, threw him bodily off his porch."

"Yeah," Balzic said. "My mother told me about that."

"Did she tell you that he never went out of the house after that? Never worked another day? And that he died less than a year later? Did she tell you that?"

"No, she didn't. But I heard it around."

"Well, do you know what Mrs. Ruffola's social security check was worth? Seventy-two dollars a month. A month, Mario! Imagine trying to live on that."

"Yeah, but—but, goddamn, Anthony, there had to be a better way."

"Sure. The Pope should auction off the Sistine Chapel. He could feed a lot of people with what he got for that."

"Aw come on, Anthony. I didn't say anything to deserve that."

"It wasn't what you said. It was your tone . . . okay, so maybe I shouldn't have made that crack. I apologize. I was out of line. But for a second there, you started to sound a little Presbyterian on me."

Balzic wheeled the cruiser over to the curb and jammed on the brakes. He twisted around to face the priest.

"What the hell is this, Anthony? We going to go through a whole thing about who's supposed to take care of the poor people, the old ladies with all their sad stories? Jesus Christ, there's a thousand stories like that around here, probably more. Anywhere there's a mine or a mill, anywhere there's widows old enough with husbands who never got in on those pension plans or got screwed out of them by some goddamn bookkeeper or lawyer—what do you got? But, goddamn it, you said there were only two women with any kind of half-decent income. Who was the other one? Sabatine's housekeeper, Mrs. Tuzzi? Well what's she going to do now? Who do you think's going to hire her again? After this gets out, who's going to give her a job? The bishop maybe?

"And what's the other one going to do, the one we took to my house a little while ago, what's she gonna do? In a couple days you're going to say the words over her income. I'm sure Abbatta had a damn good insurance policy. That printers' union took care of its own for a long time now. But tell me something, Anthony. You think she's really going to have the heart to spend any of that insurance? After what she set up with him? After tonight?"

"Mario, please don't shout, will you?" The priest opened the window and flipped out his cigarette butt. "I was just trying to suggest some of the motivation, that's all. I don't like it any better than you do. Sabatine was as far out of line as any priest can get. All I'm saying is that if you give him the benefit of some doubt, you have to recognize that he saw a chance to help some people, some old women, who really needed help, and—"

"He also saw a pretty good chance to pay off the mortgage on his church, don't forget that."

"Mario, I'm not forgetting anything," the priest said sharply. "But that man was running out of time, and who knows what was going through his head? All I'm sure about is that never, never did he think anything like this was going to happen."

"Anthony, what're you telling me, huh? For everything there's a price. You pay in money or time or sweat or blood, but you pay, and—"

"I know that, Mario," the priest said, holding up his hands as though to ward off the words.

"Let me finish," Balzic said. "When you get into a fix, when you start trying to make funny things happen, you open the door for somebody else to get in there. And, goddamn it, you know that as well as I do. The pros know it. But they know it before they start. Before they do anything, they add up the taxes they're going to pay, and they're almost a hundred percent sure who they're going to pay them to.

"But what's this amateur doing? Where'd he come from? Why the hell didn't he run a bingo game and give all those ladies a percentage? What—he was too good for bingo? He never had a game in his church as long as I can remember. If he did my mother would've been there, and so would a couple hundred other women. Bingo he can't handle. But he goes for a fix like this? With his eyes open and he doesn't even think to look? You knew who blew it for him? That poor slob Rosalie. She's the one who told Frank Dulia. She figured it. And she isn't supposed to have the brains of a cow!"

"Mario, you're shouting again."

"Anthony, two guys are—aw, fuck it. I'm sorry. I'm sorry for everybody."

"You're sorry," the priest said, laughing feebly. It was a bitter and rueful sound. "What do I tell the bishop? Never mind the bishop. What do I tell Sabatine? He doesn't know anything about this yet."

"I don't know," Balzic said, pinching the bridge of his nose as he drove away from the curb. "But maybe we ought to stop talking for a while. We're both getting a little salty."

"I'll agree with that," the priest said. "But just tell me one more thing and then I'll drop it. How did you know what Sabatine was doing?"

"Huh? Until Tullio started screaming at you, I didn't know. But that's when it all went together. My mother was the one who told me about those women winning seven hundred apiece. And something kept bugging me about that, about the amount, but I didn't even know how to think about what was bugging me until I remembered what you told me about Sabatine's mortgage payments. And even then I didn't figure it went together. But then my mother told me, tonight as a matter of fact, that Frank Dulia was Mrs. Abbatta's nephew. 'Cause at that time, right before she told me that, I was still trying to understand what Dulia said to Tullio."

"What was that?"

"He said that whatever he bet on wasn't supposed to lose. That's when I started thinking fix. But it was all a mess in my head until just a little while ago. Then when Tullio starts on you, I thought, hey, what do we got here? We got a priest, five old ladies, a linotype operator at the only newspaper in town, the paper that puts out the Treasury statement every day, and one thousand tickets at two bucks a pop. So what's the payoff on those tickets—fifteen hundred? Fourteen hundred if whoever is hustling them is greedy. You know the attraction better than I do. They pay seven hundred to one, maybe seven-fifty, which is a hell of a lot better than the five-forty a number pays.

"So if the ladies get seven hundred apiece, that leaves thirteen bills. Subtract ten bucks for printing, and that leaves twelve-ninety, which is what you said Sabatine's mortgage payments went up.

"It would've been a sweet thing," Balzic went on. "It was, until Rosalie told Dulia. And how smart could he have been? He bets with Manny. On a Treasury number! Nobody, but nobody in the world would've taken that bet except Manny. I don't know a bookmaker who would've touched it. They just don't fuck around with those things."

Balzic stretched and yawned at a stop light. "Well, I got Tullio. That's the only part of it I want. The rest is all yours. And believe me, Anthony, I don't envy you."

"Uh, Mario," the priest said hesitantly, "do I understand you? Are you saying you're not going to do anything about Sabatine?"

Balzic looked at the priest. "Anthony, you really surprise me. What do you want, huh? What am I supposed to do, huh? I mean, I know what I'd like to do. I'd like to go kick Sabatine in the ass even if he does have the big casino. But you didn't really think I was going to bust him? The women too? Ho, man, for what? Fraud? Who made the complaint? Uh-uh, Anthony, they're all yours. And if I'm you, I'd just hand it over to the bishop. I'd just dump it on his desk; let him figure it out. That's all you're supposed to do, right? Isn't that all he wants from you? A report?"

"Yeah. A report," the priest said. "It'll be the hardest thing I ever did."

A FIX LIKE THIS

Balzic drove away from the intersection slowly and pulled into the hospital parking lot. "Well, Father, you got two masses to say in the next couple days. I don't think either one of them's going to be what I'd call easy."

"No, they won't. But Sabatine's still alive." The priest got out and started for his car, but stopped after a few steps and came back.

"What's the matter?" Balzic said.

"Your cigarettes. Here." The priest handed them in.

"You want a couple to hold you?"

"Just one. I'll stop someplace and get some. Muscotti's will still be open. I could use a little wine. Maybe even a little competition with the cards."

"Yeah. Well. Maybe I'll stop down myself."

Balzic didn't stop at Muscotti's. He didn't go home either. He didn't want to discuss Father Sabatine with Father Marrazo anymore, and he knew that if he went to Muscotti's they would inevitably begin to fret and fume over the whole sorry business again. And if he went home he would have Mrs. Abbatta and Rosalie to contend with, and he didn't want any part of that either. He didn't even want to know whether his mother and Ruth were handling that well or whether they had had to be reinforced by his daughters.

He drove aimlessly around town for more than an hour, then finally turned the cruiser in the direction of his station, knowing that he was copping out on his family, but he didn't care because he made himself not want to care. He had had enough. All he wanted now was a cot in one of his lockups and a little bourbon out of the pint he kept in his desk for just such times as these, times, as he usually thought of them, when he wanted to become a bug.

Inside the duty room he asked Royer if the booking and

arraignment of Tullio Manditti had gone smoothly and correctly.

"Here's copies if you want to read them," Royer replied.

"Did you read them?"

Royer nodded.

"Any mistakes?"

"I couldn't see any."

"Is he down at Southern Regional?"

"Yeah, county guys took him."

"What was the bond?"

"Hundred thousand."

"Well, then he stays until the trial. Nobody he knows is gonna put up ten percent of that. Good. That settles it. We got the bum, we got the motive, we got the witness, and we got the bond."

"We got a witness? Who? I didn't know we had a witness."

"I didn't tell you that? Sure. Hell yes. A guy named Harsha. Lives right next door to Dulia. Saw the whole thing from less than twenty-five, thirty feet, unobstructed. What could be better than that?"

Balzic scratched his chest, pulled his underwear loose from his crotch, and went back to his office, returning in moments with the pint of bourbon. He went toward the door leading to the stairs down to the lockups. "There's nobody down there, right?"

"Not yet," Royer said.

"Well, I'm going to sleep down there. So don't let anybody bring anybody in. Tell 'em to give 'em a lecture and send 'em home. And if anybody calls, unless it's a nuclear attack, I ain't here."

"Okay, Mario. I don't know how you can sleep on those things."

"Hey, Joe, you're not insinuating that we don't provide adequate facilities for our, uh, wayward citizens, are you?"

"Who? Me?"

"Listen, if it's good enough for the rabble, it's good enough for the rousters . . . you know, sometimes I think it ought to be part of the training for the rousters to spend a couple nights in the slammer, and, oh, would it ever be good for the DAs and the judges, and man, oh, man, wouldn't it be terrific for all them fuckin' politicians? Huh? Think of it, Joe. As a requirement for public office, the first thing you had to do after you got elected was spend a weekend in the slam. Man, oh, man, wouldn't those fuckers think a little bit about some of the laws they write? Huh? Wouldn't they now? . . ."

"I don't know if I'd go that far," Royer said.

"Yeah? Well, once I read about a Jap. He built himself a coffin, and every once in a while he used to sleep in it, you know, just to get used to the notion. I think that's a hell of an idea. And that's why I sleep downstairs sometimes. You know, to get used to the notion."

"Well, it's your back," Royer said. "Sleep easy." He turned back to his desk and picked up the newspaper. "I didn't know we had a witness," he said, speaking more to himself than to Balzic.

"Well we do," Balzic said, starting down the steps. "And it's a damn good thing, 'cause if we didn't—well, I don't even want to think about that."

Balzic slept well indeed. And he hadn't needed more than two swallows of bourbon to get him started. When he woke, he accidentally kicked over the paper cup out of which he'd been drinking, and he saw with some surprise how little he had drunk.

He went to the end of the corridor to the shower room, undressed, relieved himself, and showered and shaved. He almost didn't mind putting on the same clothes, he felt so rested and refreshed. When he came up the stairs and walked into the duty room, he was humming.

"Mornin', Angelo," he said to Desk Sergeant Angelo Clemente. "What're you looking so sour about? Christ, man, look outside. It looks like spring for sure. Look at it."

"Yeah," Clemente said. "It might look good to you and me, but it ain't going to look too good to some people."

"Why? What happened? Something happen?"

"Four guys in a wildcat mine out in Westfield Township. Two guys got out, but two of them didn't."

"When'd this happen?"

"Well, the story I get from Eddie Sitko is they were just going to work. They just started in the shaft when the roof let go. They weren't fifty, sixty feet in."

Balzic shook his head and looked at his shoes for a long time, struggling not to remember what had happened to his own father. He could have walked on the ceiling more easily. "Well, that happens, Angelo," he said finally. "That happens a lot with those small outfits. Sometimes they just try to cut the costs too much. They from here?"

"Nah. Both fatals were from Westfield Township. All four of them were. I never heard the names though. Couple of good hunkies. One of them had a wife and five kids. Smolensky. George John, forty-six. The other one didn't have no family. And it might've been time for him. He was sixty-four. Harsha."

Balzic had started to walk back to his office, shaking his head in that immediate gut commiseration he felt for anyone who died as his father had. He stopped as though stung when he heard the name Clemente had said.

"What was that other one's name?"

Clemente read it off the log to make sure. "Uh, Harsha. Andrew Theodore."

A FIX LIKE THIS

"You sure?"

"Well, that's the name I got from Eddie Sitko."

"Andrew Theodore Harsha, sixty-four, from Westfield Township?"

"Yeah. I'm telling you. What's the matter?"

Balzic let out a long groan and then kicked a metal desk and then kicked it twice more until he had put three dents in it. "Jesus fuck!" he roared.

"What's the matter? Hey, Mario, Mario, what's the matter?"

"He was our witness! I'm sorry he died. I'm sorry anybody dies that way, but Jesus fucking Christ, he was our witness!"

"What witness? What're you talking about? How come nobody tells me nothing?"

"He lived next door to Dulia. He saw Tullio kill him. You know what kind of case we got against Tullio without a witness? Without Muscotti, understand, without Muscotti's help—'cause Muscotti ain't about to help him—Tullio got cousins scattered all over western Pennsylvania, and those cousins got friends. He can come up with twenty guys who'll say he was playing cards with them or whatever they have to say for him. For crissake, I'm the only person who heard Harsha's story. He was supposed to come in today at four o'clock to make a statement, that's how sure I was—sure, my ass. That's how sloppy I was. Jesus Christ," Balzic said, holding his head, "no worse testimony in the world than secondhand testimony from a cop who got it from a guy who's dead. Agghhh, bullshit! . . ."

Balzic sat sulking at the end of the bar by the kitchen in Muscotti's. He had been drinking for nearly two hours, starting with a double whiskey and then changing to wine, chasing both with large glasses of ice water. He kept telling himself not to get drunk, at the same time telling himself there wasn't anything he'd rather do.

Muscotti's was quiet. It was midafternoon. The lunch crowd had long gone, but it was still a couple of hours before the afterwork crowd would come in. Solitary customers, the retirees, the lonely, the lushes, had drifted in and out. Now there was no one except for Balzic and Vinnie.

"Mario, you better take it easy," Vinnie said, as he poured still another double wine and refilled the other, taller glass with ice and water. "It don't look good, you know what I mean?"

"What're you worrying about, huh?"

"Hey, you know, take it easy. This ain't like you. You don't look good."

"Which is it now: *it* don't look good, or *I* don't look good?"

"Ah, you know what I mean."

"Well, what are you worried about? How I look to the public? Or how I'm gonna look to the rest of your customers? They're all fuckin' squares anyway, so what's the worry?"

Vinnie sighed and shrugged. "Well, you know."

"Yeah, sure. Well, up the squares, how's that?"

"Look, why don't you stay with the ice water for a while?" Vinnie said. "Dom'll be in in a couple minutes. You can talk it over with him. Maybe he can come up with something. But don't make a mess of yourself. That's not right."

Balzic sipped the wine, then looked at Vinnie and drank it down in four swallows. He knocked over the glass setting it on the bar. "Vinnie, we been friends too long for you to start making like a teacher with me, huh?"

Vinnie threw out his hands and let them fall against his legs. "Okay, Mario. I don't say nothing. No more."

"Then put some more in there."

"You got it, buddy. You can drink 'em all day, I can damn sure pour 'em all day."

Balzic stifled a yawn and rubbed his palms together. He spun around slowly on the stool and looked at the opposite wall, then spun back and read the community college basketball schedule for the fifth or sixth time. He took a sip of the chablis Vinnie brought him and then a sip of the ice water. A motorcycle roared by on State Street, its engine noise piercing, causing Balzic to close his eyes and cover his ears.

He felt someone tap him on the shoulder. When he opened his eyes and took his hands away from his ears, he saw Dom Muscotti and heard him saying something about ". . . arresting those friggin' nuts."

"What nuts?"

"Those motorcycle nuts. They make me crazy with all that noise. There got to be something stupid about people who like noise. Ain't there an ordinance about how much noise you can make?"

"Sure," Balzic said. "Three of them."

"Well why don't you tell your guys to enforce them?" Dom screwed up his face and walked around behind the bar. "You know what noise does to you, Mario? I been reading about it. It can send your blood pressure up twenty, thirty points, a real sudden noise, d'you know that?"

Balzic scratched his scalp, rubbed his lips, and took another sip of wine.

"Did you know that, Mario?"

"Yeah I know that. But do you know what I'd have to do to enforce any ordinance about noise? I'd have to have ten more cars and twenty more people. For crissake, I'm supposed to have two lieutenants, one for juveniles and one for administration, and I been waiting three years for Council to approve the money for them. Do I have to say any more?"

"Okay, Mario, okay. Take it easy. I was just making conversation anyway." Muscotti turned away and went through the letters and bills Vinnie had handed him. He said nothing, put the envelopes and bills in a nook beside the coffee machine, then coughed and leaned under the bar to spit in an empty beer case.

"What're you drinking for now?" Muscotti said when he straightened up. "You know, you look a little drunk."

"Your bartender been giving it to me for twenty minutes, now you're going to start. Maybe you ought to start selling candy."

"Hey, I'm sorry I asked. Just pretend I didn't say nothing, okay?"

"No, I won't," Balzic said. "You want to know what I'm drinking for, I'm going to tell you. You're just the guy who ought to hear it anyway. It was one of your *paisans*—no, not one. Three of them. First it was Manny. Then Tullio. Then Brownie for letting Tullio get away from him. And those three assholes got me in a real bind."

"Let's go in the back, huh, Mario? If you're going to drink wine, you might as well drink good stuff."

"Okay. Fine. That's fine with me. 'Cause I got plenty to say."

"Okay, okay, take it easy. Come on back and say it."

Balzic left his wine and water on the bar and followed Muscotti to the room where they'd talked before when he'd made his senseless threat to shut down Muscotti's operation. He let Muscotti go in first and then dropped woozily on a chair, running his fingers through his hair and then rubbing the back of his neck.

"Hey, Dom," he said, "no more wine for me. I had more than enough about an hour ago."

"Whatever you say," Muscotti said, sitting opposite Balzic. "So, uh, what's the problem?"

"I told you, I'm in a real bind. The worst one I ever been in."

"So tell me."

"I had a witness. He saw Tullio put the job on Dulia, watched—"

"You 'had' a witness?"

Balzic nodded and rubbed his temples. "He got killed this morning. A fuckin' mine roof caved in on him. But without him, the only case I got against Tullio is circumstantial. It's a hell of a case. Any third-rate assistant DA could nail Tullio easy."

"So what're you worrying about?"

"In order to do it that way, I got to open up a real can of worms. I'd have to bust six people, including a priest and five old ladies, for operating a lottery, for fraud, for conspiracy, that whole number. Then I'd have to get the DA, Weigh, to go along with immunity for them so they could testify about the circumstances. And, uh, in any other case, that's no big deal. But this time it might not be so easy. I don't have to tell you Weigh ain't Catholic, and he just might get a hair up his ass because this is all Catholic and it all smells.

"But forget that," Balzic went on. "I mean, even if Weigh played it straight, even if he went along with the immunity, once these people testify, they're finished. The papers, the television, the radio—they'd eat 'em alive. No matter that nobody prosecutes them, they testify and they may as well crawl in their coffins."

"Wait a minute," Muscotti said. "You lost me. What priest? What old ladies?"

"Sabatine—"

"What?" Muscotti's eyes went wide and his head jerked forward. You mean the Sabatine from out St. Jude's? The one who tried to get Weisberg in Westfield Golf Club?"

"Yeah, yeah—"

"Why, Christ, I heard he got the big casino."

"Yeah, yeah, that's him. But wait'll you hear who the ladies are. You're gonna shit. Listen to this lineup: Mrs. Motti, Mrs.

Ruffola, Mrs. Cafasso, Mrs. Tuzzi, and Mrs. Abbatta You know what they did?"

"Hey, Mario," Muscotti said, standing suddenly and folding his arms and taking a step backward. "I'm not so sure I want to know. And I don't know if you ought to be telling me."

"Yeah? Well, sit down, 'cause you're going to hear it. 'Cause your fat gofer jumped right in the middle of it. And his brother finished it last night. He killed Nick Abbatta last night—"

"What?" Muscotti had to support himself on the back of the chair he'd been sitting on.

"You heard me. So sit down and—"

"Holy shit," Muscotti said. "And this was because of what the priest done?"

"That's right. They started it, and Dulia heard about it—"

"Yeah. But, Mario, you're still talking, you're still gonna tell me about a priest, and when you start talking about a priest, there's some things you just ain't supposed to say, I don't care what he done."

"My ass. Sit down and listen. Because this priest is going to get a lot more grief if I don't come up with something, you understand?"

Muscotti scowled and chewed his lower lip and paced around the tiny room for nearly a minute. At last he sat and nodded. "All right. I'm listening."

"Okay, so here it is. Now I don't know whose idea it was in the beginning. I don't care. It doesn't matter anyway. But Sabatine went for a lottery. You know the kind, off the Treasury balance at two bucks a throw on a thousand tickets. Then somebody convinces Nick Abbatta to rig the numbers to match up with one of the ones those old ladies had. The women got seven bills apiece when it was their turn to win—or maybe they split it every month, I don't know—but the rest of it went on St. Jude's mortgage. Anyway, Abbatta's sister, the retarded one? Rosalie?"

Dom nodded vigorously. "I know her."

"Well, somehow she put it together. With her brains, I can't see how, but she did. What I figure is everybody was doing a lot of talking about it in front of her, figuring, you know, what does she know? But it turns out she worshipped Dulia, and she spilled it to him, or maybe just told him enough so he could figure the rest out for himself. But he couldn't have been too smart because you know who he booked it with."

Muscotti held up his right hand. "Say no more, Mario. I got it figured from there . . . boy, I see what you mean. This could really stink. And that friggin' Weigh, he collects taxes from me like two sponges. He charges me twice as much as Froggy used to. It took him two years to get around to it. Christ, I have to laugh now. I remember thinking, son of a gunsky, hey, maybe this Weigh is really an honest square. But, boy, when he got around to it, he really put it to me. And I can't get a goddamn thing on him. I been trying ever since I started to pay, but he's smart, that bastard. Someday, remind me to tell you the ways I got to wash the money before he touches it . . . but never mind that. The important thing, Mario, is you're right. There's no doubt, he's a friggin' Mason all right. He'd love this. He'd prosecute it all by himself. He wouldn't let no assistant get the glory. That fucker'd have it both ways. He'd have my money and he'd be laughing at all us Micks."

Dom paused and shook his head harder and harder as though trying to resolve something very difficult. "That fat-ass. What's my mother got to like him for, can you tell me that? He got more fat between his ears than he got anyplace else. But she likes him. She really does. She calls him twice a day in the hospital. She must've sent him three baskets of fruit already . . . I'm stuck, Mario. I can't do nothing to him. You got to understand that. She'd never forgive me. And I couldn't handle that."

"Okay. So we got your mother and Manny on one side. But what do we got on the other side? Huh? Six widows and a priest with cancer."

"Six? I thought five."

"What's Dulia's wife? Don't she qualify?"

"Okay, okay." Muscotti held up his hands. He stuck his lower lip out and rubbed it thoughtfully with his index finger. "Okay," he said slowly, "okay. I can handle it. I paid enough taxes down that friggin' courthouse. But, Mario, you got to understand, I can't let Manny take too much weight. He can't do no more than three months. My mother can handle that. I'll talk to her. She'll understand that much. But, uh, one thing. Whoever I get, you got to school him. You can't let nobody else do it. It got to be right."

"Don't worry," Balzic said. "I'll make him a genius."

Tullio Manditti was brought into courtroom number four of the Conemaugh County courthouse five weeks to the day after Nicolao Abbatta Jr. was buried, five weeks and a day after Francis Dulia was buried.

There were few spectators in the room and no reporters. Tullio's trial had been docketed for the fall session of criminal court, but for reasons Clerk of Courts Louis Cepola wouldn't have explained to Jesus if He'd come back, the trial was suddenly called for the last day of the spring session. In fact, only Cepola, presiding Judge J. Harold Corcoran, Assistant District Attorney Ralph Manganero, Defense Attorney Louis Harmonich, the witnesses, the prospective jurors, the bailiffs and other court officers, and two spectators knew it was to be a trial. Tullio kept leaning over to his lawyer during jury selection and whispering hoarsely, "How come they're picking a jury? I thought this was supposed to be the preliminary hearing."

"I already told you," Louis Harmonich said back each time, "you already had one of those."

"So how come I wasn't here?" Tullio snapped during the last of these exchanges.

"You didn't have to be here. I was here, Mr. Mandizzi. That was enough."

"How many times I got to tell you? My name ain't Mandizzi! It's Manditti. Ditti. Like ditto, only with an 'i' on the end."

Harmonich shrugged sheepishly.

Balzic, sitting in the first row between Father Marrazo and Dom Muscotti, leaned over to Muscotti and whispered, "Who found that guy?"

"Corcoran," Muscotti whispered back. "D'you think the Pope?"

"He must've had help."

"What help? That guy was sitting in the public defender's office like an apple waiting to fall off a tree."

"Oh yeah?"

"Certainly. Been in court about three times, all for drunk driving. Flunked the bar exam twice. Finished fifth from last in his class."

"And Corcoran found him all by himself, huh?"

"So? He was looking. What can I tell you?"

Balzic shook his head.

"What's the matter? Even Tullio's entitled to a lawyer. So what's a judge supposed to do if all the other lawyers are busy? He got to appoint one. So he appointed one."

Jury selection took three hours, two before lunch and one after. Court reconvened at exactly one-fifteen—when Judge Corcoran said it would—and the bailiffs and court stenographer were so surprised by Corcoran's attack of punctuality they had to be phoned twice in the basement coffee shop by Corcoran's tipstaff before they believed it. At one-nineteen, when they hurried in, Corcoran had been on the bench turning his gavel end over end for four minutes.

At two-nineteen, the last alternate juror was picked, the jury was sworn, and then Corcoran began to explain their duties and responsibilities. He was just at the point where he usually became loquacious, the point where he usually told juries how the whole system of American justice was based on the common wisdom of twelve ordinary citizens reasoning together, when he and everyone else in the room heard the insistent rapping of metal on wood coming from the first row of the spectators' section to Balzic's immediate left.

Balzic glanced over in time to see Muscotti putting a quarter in his pocket.

Corcoran coughed, drank some water, apologized for the laryngitis he felt coming on, and said, "Just pay attention to the evidence you hear. That's all that counts. The evidence. I'll tell you what you're supposed to do later on. Mr. Manganero, Mr. Harmonich, are you ready?"

Both attorneys stood and said they were, and then both waived making an opening statement.

Manganero began the case for the Commonwealth of Pennsylvania by calling Dr. Aram Sharma, the Indian Balzic remembered as the doctor who had been on duty when Frank Dulia was brought into the Emergency Unit of Conemaugh General Hospital. Dr. Sharma referred constantly to a small note pad, describing vividly in precise English in both medical and layman's language Dulia's condition when he had examined him.

Louis Harmonich said he had no questions.

Manganero next called the Lebanese doctor, who told of witnessing Dulia's death and filling out the death certificate.

Louis Harmonich said again that he had no questions.

Manganero next called Coroner Wallace Grimes and led him through a series of questions designed to illuminate Grimes' qualifications in forensic pathology. Louis Harmonich interrupted him to say that that wasn't necessary. "Everybody knows Dr. Grimes' reputation."

"All right, Dr. Grimes," Manganero said. "Did you perform an autopsy on one Francis Dulia sometime during the early morning hours of March 24?"

"I did."

"And would you tell us the cause of Mr. Dulia's death?"

"Massive brain damage as a direct result of multiple fractures of the left parietal and left temporal bones." Grimes did not have to refer to his own report, which lay in his lap, nor did he have to be instructed to indicate on his own head for the jury's benefit exactly what he was talking about.

"Where there other bruises or fractures or marks on the deceased's body, Doctor?"

"There were. Many of them." Grimes went on to enumerate the fractures. "There were no abrasions or lacerations. Just contusions. No cuts or burns. Just swellings."

"What would cause that, Doctor? In your expert opinion, what would cause the sort of injury to a human body such as you've described?"

"Well, the body is struck with some instrument which has been padded, something like a baseball bat that's been wrapped with a towel. The body receives the blow without suffering laceration or abrasion, but if the blow is powerful enough, something has to give somewhere, and what usually happens is that a bone fractures."

Manganero then repeated all the fractures that Grimes had enumerated previously, asking after each one if Grimes would say that that particular fracture was caused in the manner he'd just described. Grimes agreed after each one that it had.

Louis Harmonich said he had no questions.

Manganero called Balzic next. Right after he asked Balzic to identify himself, Louis Harmonich stood and said that there was no need to elaborate on Balzic's background or on his integrity. "Everybody knows who he is."

Balzic had to look at his shoes to keep his nervous smile from being seen by the jury.

Manganero led Balzic through a series of questions which focused on and skirted the periphery of the fact that Francis Dulia had been transported to the hospital in a pickup truck owned and driven by one Andrew T. Harsha, since deceased, who had witnessed something in the backyard of his neighbor's—Mr. Dulia's—house on the afternoon of March 23.

Manganero began to ask Balzic what it was that Mr. Harsha had witnessed, but Louis Harmonich objected, saying that though Balzic's testimony was obviously the best evidence since Mr. Harsha was dead, it was still second-hand evidence and he wanted the court to instruct the jury in that regard. Judge Corcoran looked sternly at Harmonich and was about to reply to his objection when Manganero said, "It's all right, your honor. We have another witness. I have no more questions for this witness."

Louis Harmonich said he too had no questions for this witness.

"Step down, Chief," Judge Corcoran said.

"Call Mr. Domenic Scalzo," Manganero said.

Dom "Soup" Scalzo passed Balzic on his way to the witness chair as though he had never seen him before in his life. He said, "I do," before the clerk finished reading the oath and took the witness chair with his eyes fixed on Manganero. He looked at no one else while he spoke.

"Mr. Scalzo," Manganero began, "would you state your full name and address and give your occupation?"

"Domenic G. Scalzo. I live at 531 Theobald Avenue, Rocksburg. I'm self-employed."

"At, uh, what are you self-employed, Mr. Scalzo?"

"I'm a business consultant."

"Could you be more precise than that?"

"I advise people about investments and what their chances are of making a profit."

Judge Corcoran had a coughing fit, interrupting Scalzo's testimony for almost a minute.

"Uh, Mr. Scalzo," Manganero said after Corcoran managed to get control of himself, "did you happen to be in the residence of one Andrew T. Harsha, now deceased, on the afternoon of March 23?"

"I was."

"What were you doing there?"

"I was advising Mr. Harsha on an investment he wanted to make. If he'd've listened to me, he'd still be alive today."

"And what was that?"

"I told him to get out of that mine he was in. I told him he was getting too old for that kind of work. It was all right to own a part of it, but he shouldn't be working in it."

"Yes. Well, unfortunately, Mr. Harsha did not take your advice. We all know that he died in that very mine one day later. Well, Mr. Scalzo, will you please tell us if you saw anything unusual that day while you were visiting and advising Mr. Harsha?"

"Yes. I did. I mean, I will. We were in the kitchen having a drink. He just came home from the mine, and he said he wanted to cut the dust a little...."

Balzic could stand to listen to no more. He bumped

Muscotti's knee with his own and waved his hand feebly from side to side to show that he was leaving. He had to step in front of Father Marrazo to get to the aisle. The priest looked up at him, and his eyes were disturbingly hard and disbelieving. Balzic rushed from the courtroom, looking at the carpet, avoiding everyone's eyes.

Outside in the corridor, Balzic went to the marble balustrade overlooking the circular stairwell which was directly under the dome of the courthouse. He looked up at the dome and fumbled to loosen his tie and unbutton his collar. He felt himself breathing rapidly and tried to take long, slow breaths. He licked his upper lip and tasted perspiration. He looked at his palms, and they glistened wet in the light of the great globe suspended from the center of the dome.

Someone touched his arm, and Balzic swung his head around so quickly that he nearly became dizzy. It was Father Marrazo.

"Mario," the priest began and then stopped as though he had no idea what he was going to say, but his gaze was so intense that Balzic had to turn away. "Mario, what's—what the hell is going on?"

Balzic leaned his backside against the balustrade to support himself and jerked at his tie and collar. "You know what's going on, so what're you asking for?"

"I don't know," the priest said. "I sat in there and I listened and I couldn't believe what I was listening to. And then you jumped up and your face was white. Mario, I want you to tell me what's going on."

Balzic started to walk away from the priest, but Father Marrazo caught him by the sleeve. "Mario, I've never interfered with you before, and I may not know everything you know, and I may be way out of line, but I know when something is wrong, and there is something really wrong going on in there." The priest was trying to whisper, but his words sounded to Balzic as though he were shouting.

"Aaagh," Balzic growled. "What the hell did you want to go on, huh?"

"The right thing."

"I did the right thing. What do you think I did?"

"Mario, you may think you did the right thing, but it's coming out all wrong. The way you're doing it is all wrong."

"And how 'bout if I did it the right way, huh? I could've done it that way, sure. But do you know Weigh's a Mason? Huh? Do you know—"

"I don't care what he is. That doesn't change anything."

"I don't believe this," Balzic said. "I don't believe this is you talking. After all you know?"

"You don't believe it? Huh? You don't believe it's me? Then what're you doing out here with sweat all over your face? Look at me. You can't even look at me. And you talk about after all I know? That's right, that's right. I hear Mrs. Abbatta's confession every day. The others, two, three times a week. And I heard Sabatine's. He asked for me. He could've asked for the bishop. I wish he had. But I was with him right up to the end and I heard him. Which means I heard everything. But what I haven't heard is what Soup is doing on that witness chair." The priest's face was flushed, and the veins stood out on his forehead and throat from trying to whisper while talking so forcefully.

Balzic took a long time before he answered. As many ways as he thought to say it, he knew finally that it didn't matter how he said it. He could give only one answer. "I know where the confessional is."

"Okay," Father Marrazo said. "Okay . . . okay. . . ." He repeated that word several more times as though trying to find satisfaction in its mere repetition. He cleared his throat and tugged at his own collar. Then he looked at his shoes. "You, uh, you want to go, uh, get some wine? Huh?"

Balzic nodded slowly. "Right now I could drink just about all the wine there is in the world."

They walked in silence to Muscotti's and did not speak to each other until they began to quibble over who was going to pay for the drinks. What little conversation there was took place between Balzic and Vinnie who kept demanding to be brought up to date on the trial. He couldn't understand why they'd both left if it had not yet gone to the jury. Neither Balzic nor Father Marrazo would answer that.

Their drinking was joyless, mechanical, a seeking after the alcohol rather than the wine. It took nearly an hour before they started to feel the wine flowing in them, and by that time they were threatening to drink all the chablis and chianti Vinnie had on the shelves. Balzic even started making noises about going to the backroom to help himself to Muscotti's private stock of Valpolicella.

Mila Sanders Rizzo, sighing giddily, came in then and plopped down on the stool next to Balzic. She leaned close to him and whispered, "I understand you solved your problem."

"Well, that depends," Balzic said, glancing uncomfortably at Father Marrazo. "In a way I did, and then again I didn't. How you coming with yours?"

"Well, I guess that depends too. Dom wants me to manage a store for him."

Balzic started to smile. "What kind of store?"

"Oh, this woman's husband died, and she's sick and she wants to get rid of it. Dom says there's a real market for what they sell." She was smiling impishly, sardonically. She leaned close to him again and whispered, "Religious supplies. Bibles and crucifixes and plaster saints and rosaries and medals and bumper stickers that say all kinds of goopy stuff like, 'God's only dead if you're Red,' and crap like that. Dom says with all the halos I see on people I'd make a million dollars in ten years. I told him I'd do it if he let me put up a big yellow neon cross with a sign on it that said, 'Two million rosaries sold.' You know, like hamburgers. Boy, did he get mad."

Balzic nodded as though it was all the most reasonable thing he'd heard in weeks. "What's his wife say?"

"Oh, you don't think he talked to her about it, do you?" she said, pulling back and laughing loud.

Before Balzic could reply Dom Scalzo barged through the front door, scowling and cursing under his breath until he drew even with Balzic's back. Then he tapped Balzic on the back and started to speak but he was too furious. For some moments all he could do was curse.

"What's the matter with you?" Balzic said. "You just did the good deed of your life and you look like you just got robbed."

"I'll tell you what's the matter," Scalzo said. "You wanna hear what's the matter? I'm gonna tell you what's the matter. Jimmie Salio, that bastard—Corcoran's bailiff?"

"I know who he is. Who doesn't?"

"Yeah, well, he thinks it's a big joke. I come down off the stand and I start to walk out. I'm done, what am I gonna stick around for? He's standing back there at the back door and he's looking at his watch. I'm almost past him, and he grabs me and he whispers—you know how he whispers? Like normal people talk that's how he whispers—he whispers, 'You stopped testifying at exactly four-twenty-eight.' And then he hands me six bucks and he whispers again, 'A buck around. Four-twenty-eight. On the new stock.' So I'm going, no, no, you know. I'm shaking my head and I'm not taking the money. So the cocksucker—excuse my language, Father—so the dumb bastard shoves the money in my coat pocket. So whatta you think? Don't you know there's a state cop sitting right there, right in the last row, and he hears everything. And he follows me outside, and Jimmie's following me and I'm trying to give the money back to Jimmie and that goddamn state cop arrests me! Right there in the hall! Jesus Christ, I wanna throw both them bastards right over the balcony.

"I go in there to do something good for once in my life, for justice—for justice, you goddamn Mario, ain't that what you told me? For justice I go in there and tell the biggest lie I ever told in my life and now I'm under arrest for bookin'. Stick your justice up your ass."

Balzic turned to Father Marrazo and both of them looked at Vinnie and then all three roared with laughter until tears were streaming down their cheeks.

"Oh, God, God," Balzic said at last, his eyes, mouth, and stomach aching from laughter. "Vinnie, give him a drink. Give everybody a drink. And keep them coming. I got everybody's."

And Vinnie did. He said later on when he told the story that he'd never poured so many drinks or laughed so hard in an hour's time in his life, and no one who had been there that day ever doubted him. Just as no one ever doubted him when he said that the next day he laughed even harder when Dom Muscotti told Soup Scalzo that he had put Jimmie Salio up to it, had told him to have someone else tip off a state cop and make sure he was there in the last row, and that it was he himself who had given Salio the six dollars Salio kept trying to force on Soup.

"You should've seen Soup's face," Vinnie would tell the story time and again. "Oh Christ, I thought he was gonna choke. All he could say was, 'Why? What'd you want to go and do that to me for?' And Dom looked at him and said, 'Soup, I knew how you were gonna think when you came down out of the chair. Like you did something really good. And you did. But I didn't want you to start thinking you were too good. You start thinking you're too good, you're gonna forget who you are.'"

And no one laughs harder at that story than Balzic.

ABOUT THE AUTHOR

Carl Constantine Kosak (1934–2023), better known as acclaimed mystery writer K.C. Constantine, is famed for his mysteries featuring Mario Balzic. Constantine showed much more interest in the characters in his novels than the actual mystery, and his later novels became ever more philosophical, threatening to leave the mystery genre behind completely. In 1989, Constantine was nominated for the Edgar Allan Poe Award for Best Novel for *Joey's Case*. Despite his success, he managed to keep his literary identity completely hidden until 2011 when he appeared in person for the first time at the annual Festival of Mystery hosted by Mystery Lovers Bookshop in Oakmont.

THE MARIO BALZIC MYSTERIES

FROM MYSTERIOUSPRESS.COM
AND OPEN ROAD MEDIA

MYSTERIOUSPRESS.COM

MYSTERIOUSPRESS.COM

Otto Penzler, owner of the Mysterious Bookshop in Manhattan, founded the Mysterious Press in 1975. Penzler quickly became known for his outstanding selection of mystery, crime, and suspense books, both from his imprint and in his store. The imprint was devoted to printing the best books in these genres, using fine paper and top dust-jacket artists, as well as offering many limited, signed editions.

Now the Mysterious Press has gone digital, publishing ebooks through **MysteriousPress.com**.

MysteriousPress.com offers readers essential noir and suspense fiction, hard-boiled crime novels, and the latest thrillers from both debut authors and mystery masters. Discover classics and new voices, all from one legendary source.

FIND OUT MORE AT
WWW.MYSTERIOUSPRESS.COM

FOLLOW US:
@emysteries and Facebook.com/MysteriousPressCom

MysteriousPress.com is one of a select group of publishing partners of Open Road Integrated Media, Inc.

THe MYSTeRIOUS BOOKSHOP, founded in 1979, is located in Manhattan's Tribeca neighborhood. It is the oldest and largest mystery-specialty bookstore in America.

The shop stocks the finest selection of new mystery hardcovers, paperbacks, and periodicals. It also features a superb collection of signed modern first editions, rare and collectable works, and Sherlock Holmes titles. The bookshop issues a free monthly newsletter highlighting its book clubs, new releases, events, and recently acquired books.

58 Warren Street
info@mysteriousbookshop.com
(212) 587-1011
Monday through Saturday
11:00 a.m. to 7:00 p.m.

FIND OUT MORE AT:

www.mysteriousbookshop.com

FOLLOW US:

@TheMysterious and Facebook.com/MysteriousBookshop

Find a full list of our authors and
titles at www.openroadmedia.com

FOLLOW US
@OpenRoadMedia